JAYNE'S INTELL REVIEW PD

THE HAVENITE REPUBLICAN NAVY

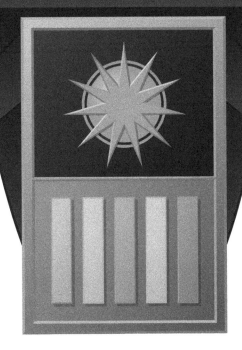

David Weber,
Ken Burnside
and Thomas Pope

Contributors
Don Beseny, Joe Buckley, John Lerchey, Thomas Marrone, Steve Osmanski, Giles Schildt, Marcus Wilmes

Artwork
Jenny Dolfen, Thomas Marrone, Charles Oines

Special thanks to
David Weber and Chris Roensch

Final Sword Productions

P.O. Box 389
Pelican Rapids, MN 56572
www.finalswordproductions.com
(218) 863-1784

TABLE OF CONTENTS

THE PEOPLE'S REPUBLIC OF HAVEN

The Haven System lies 667 light years from Old Earth, roughly 155 light years further away than the Manticore Binary System. In spite of this greater distance, the first shuttle that landed on its habitable planet (also called Haven) did so on 6/30/1309 P.D., over a century before Landing Day on Manticore. This discrepancy is explained by the introduction of the Warshawski Sail, which revolutionized the logistics of colonization, just as it had every other aspect of interstellar movement.

Haven's primary is a slightly brighter G-class star than Sol, as a result, Haven's orbit is farther out, and the local year is 15% longer than Earth's. The local planetary rotational period (or sidereal day) is 24.56 standard hours in length, and the local year (solar orbital period) is 412.25 local days. The Havenite planetary calendar is divided into 13 months, 9 with 32 days each, and 4 of 31 days each. The short months are on the 3rd, 5th, 10th and 12th months. Every 4 years, the third month gains a leap day, becoming 32 days long; every 320 planetary years, the leap day is skipped as a calendar adjustment.

Like the Star Kingdom of Manticore, the Havenite clock uses a partial hour called "Comp" for timekeeping to reconcile the extra minutes in the Havenite day.

From a planetographic perspective, Haven is remarkably Earthlike, with an axial tilt that generates seasons, but keeps them in moderation. It receives slightly more instellation from its primary than Earth does, but high cloud cover makes the climate differences negligible. Surface gravity was close enough to Earth's standard G as to be unremarkable. Like the vast majority of planets in this part of the galactic neighborhood, Haven's biochemistry has right handed chirality. Some instances of allergies have been reported, but routine medical practices made this negligible. Importing terrestrial agricultural life forms was straightforward; most terrestrial crops were unappealing to local vermin.

Astrographically speaking, the Haven system is in an attractive stellar neighborhood, with a high concentration of F, G, and K class stars with the telltale signs of potential water worlds. The founding expedition to Haven was financed as a joint venture by no fewer than eleven corporations based on member planets of the Solarian League, and was quite well funded. It also had the advantage of Warshawski-sail transport of future generations of colonists and emergency relief supplies. A powerful public relations campaign touted the nearly idyllic climate and vast expanses of cheap, arable land to move to on Haven, and Haven pulled colonists from several Solarian League worlds. Facilitated by the new hypership technology, Haven grew at incredible speed. By 1430 P.D, barely 120 T-years after Landing, the Republic of Haven already boasted a planetary population of greater than 900 million. As part of their planetary centennial celebrations, the Republic of Haven announced that it was mounting colonization expeditions of its own. Haven's vibrant political system and booming economy lent the astrographic neighborhood the name "The Haven Sector", in spite of the fact that six other systems in the same region had been colonized before, or almost simultaneously with Haven.

By 1475, the Havenite economy and government had proven themselves extremely efficient and effective. Politically, Haven was a representative republic with a strong and politically active middle class, and its economic policy enshrined the principles of liberal capitalism with minimal governmental interference. Coupled with the "jump start" provided by the colony's highly favorable initial circumstances, this combination of market efficiency and flexible government created a planetary standard of living greater than most Solarian League member worlds, and it became the envy and the pattern for every other world in its part of space.

Over the next two centuries, Haven strove to, and mostly succeeded, in fulfilling its promise, rising to a system population of almost seven billion and becoming an interstellar Athens. The Haven Sector, although composed of independent worlds and star systems, was second only to the Solarian League in economic power, and its robust politics and vibrant and expansive economic policy gave it, functionally, a "youthful vigor". This contrasted with the satisfied contentment of much of the Solarian League, which had slid into introspective politics rather than expansion, leaving the outlying Sectors to varying levels of neglect.

Although the Haven Sector contained no wormhole junctions, it was within close transit to the Manticore Wormhole Junction, and from there to the League. (Discovery of the Trevor's Star terminus in the 17th century PD, shortened the travel times even further.) There was every reason to believe that Haven's expansion and prosperity would continue.

Tragically, it did not. Precise identification of a specific event which caused the change within the sector is impossible, though there are several competing theories. The most prominent of the theories can be called, in general terms, a case of over-achievement. Haven, and the sector, had done too well. Haven's capitalistic drive and élan had amassed incalculable wealth, and with it, a society stratified on economic means, where the disparity between the richest and poorest became a gulf. Cries for social justice and more even distribution of the wealth were mounted, and used to mobilize blocs of "poor" voters. Even though the poorest members of Haven's society were immeasurably better off than, say the pre-Anderman citizens of New Berlin, they were not well off compared to their own affluent neighbors, and relative poverty always casts a jealous eye at those with more.

With the mobilization of economic disparatism in its electorate, the Republic began to experiment, cautiously at first, with assistance and welfare programs to increase the opportunities of its less advantaged citizens. Always for the best of intentions, these plans were meant to give hope to the downtrodden, to free those who were in poverty's grimmest grip, and put them on the road to opportunity. Unfortunately, over years and decades, what began as an experiment became something else. It became politically difficult to campaign for fiscal responsibility on social programs, then nearly suicidal. Transfer payments became increasingly important for the maintenance of the working poor, requiring greater levies on the productive elements of society. The overhead of these transfer payments proved to be a crippling cost – of every credit allocated to transfer payments, 60 percent was consumed in overhead. Marginal industrial operations were shored up by protective tariffs, government loans, and outright grants to encourage full employment, which both undercut the overall

SOUTHWEST HAVEN QUADRANT - 1905 PD

PEOPLE'S REPUBLIC FLAG

Secour

Helmsport

Cascabel

Hyacinth

Hannah's Star

Yalta

Franconia

Lowell

Sun-yat

Runciman

Suchien

Seljuk

Samson

Reiko

Santander

Owens

Barnett

Madras

Seaford 9

Poicters

Talbot

Mylar

Hancock

Sallah

Seabring

Yorik

Mendoza

Corrigan

Welladay

Chelsea

Zanzibar

Alizon

Klein Station

Adler

Mathias

Talisman

Clairmont

Barnes

Endicott

Micah

Quest

Allman

Yeltsin

Treadway

Casca

Manticore

Clearaway

Candor

Zuckerman

Minette

Elric

Dorcas

KEY

Ramon

Major Base

Manticoran Alliance

People's Republic of Haven

Quentin

Neutral

Grendelsbane

Solway

PRH
Sphere of Influence

*Radii indicate the distance a
modern warship can travel in
a standard day. (~8.21 LY)*

0 Light Years (LY)   50 LY   100 LY

efficiency and productivity of the industrial base and encouraged rampant inflation. Inflation further worsened the condition of the poor, requiring still higher transfer payments—payments which were soon adjusted for inflation on a mandated basis—and, as the network of assistance proliferated, it came to be seen as a fundamental "right" of those receiving the aid.

By 1680 P.D., Haven had issued its famous "Economic Bill of Rights," declaring that all of its citizens had an "unalienable right" to a relative standard of living to be defined (and adjusted as inflation required) by statute by the House of Legislators. While lauded as a humanitarian aim, it proved disastrous for the economy.

In the process, the government had initiated an unending spiral of inflation, higher transfer payments, and increasing deficit spending. Moreover, it had (quite unintentionally, at least at first) undermined the fundamental strength of its own democracy. The middle class, the traditional backbone of the Republic, was under increasing pressure from both above and below, caught in the squeeze between inflation and ever larger levies against its earnings to support the welfare system. Whereas the middle class had once seen the upper class as (at worst) essentially friendly rivals or (at best) allies in their joint prosperity, they came to see the wealthy, as did the poor, as enemies, fighting over the scraps of a dwindling prosperity. Worse, the middle class's traditional aspiration to upward mobility had become a vanishingly remote dream, as the inflation rate undermined savings and capitalization of businesses. As more small businesses floundered, taking banks down with them, more regulations were put on the books to keep banks from writing risky loans, and those aspiring in the middle class to rise in prosperity by hard work and innovation found more roadblocks to their ambitions. For the middle class, it became much easier to focus resentment on those who had more than they, particularly when stymied by bureaucratic road blocks, than on those who had less—a tendency which became ever more pronounced as "enlightened" commentators and academics secured dominant positions in the media and educational system.

Perhaps worst of all, was the evolution of the "Dolist" blocs. The Dolists (so called because they were "on the dole," receiving government assistance to greater or lesser degree) were still franchised voters and, quite logically, supported the candidates who offered them the most. What had originally been grass roots activism to bring enlightenment to the plight of the poor had turned into systematized self-interest, and the Dolists' self-interest interlocked with that of increasingly careerist politicians. A new class of machine politicians, the "Dolist managers," emerged, playing the role of king-makers by delivering huge blocs of votes to chosen candidates. Incumbent politicians realized that their continued incumbency was virtually assured with the managers' backing—and that the converse was also true. A politician targeted by the "People's Quorum" (the official term for the alliance of Dolist managers) was doomed, and as they became aware of their power, the leaders of the Quorum selected specific politicians to punish as an example of the electoral power the Quorum represented.

Regrettably, and nearly unbelievably to many, and symptomatic of something just short of system-wide mass insanity, most of those who recognized that something was wrong embraced a "conspiracy theory" which assumed that their problems must result from someone's hostile machinations—probably the domestic "monied classes" or foreign industries who "dumped" their cheap, shoddy products on the Havenite economy. As bad, and arguably worse, the malaise of economic reapportionment

had turned the vibrant, minimal interference capitalism that had given Haven its wealth into a guilt about anything resembling capitalistic enterprise. This led to an entrenched element of "this wouldn't be happening to us if we weren't somehow at fault" in the vast majority of mid-18th century Havenite political and societal analysis and rhetoric, and this masochistic tendency only became more pronounced as the century wound to a close.

By 1750 P.D., the Republic—no longer "The Republic of Haven," but now "The People's Republic of Haven"—had become the captive of a coalition of professional politicians (indeed, politicians who had never had and were not qualified for any other career) and the Quorum, aided and abetted by a morally and intellectually bankrupt academic community and a mass media philosophically at home with the Quorum's objectives and cowed (where necessary) by threats of blacklisting. That the Quorum could succeed in blacklisting journalists had been demonstrated in 1746 P.D. in the case of Adele Wasserman, one of the last moderate journalists. Her moderation, which was actually a bit left of center by mid-17th century standards, was labeled "conservative" or, more frequently, "reactionary" by her 18th century contemporaries. She herself was called "an enemy of the common man," "a slave of the monied powers," and (most cutting slur then available on Haven) "a fiscal elitist," and her employer, one of the last independent press services, was pressured into terminating her contract (for "socially insensitive and inappropriate demagoguery") by means of an economic boycott, strikes, and governmental pressure. Her firing, followed by her subsequent relocation to the Kingdom of Manticore and a successful career as a leading theorist of the Centrist Party, was the writing on the wall for any who had eyes. Unless something quite extraordinary and even more unlikely intervened, the current Havenite system was doomed.

The problem, of course, was one which had arisen as long ago as Old Earth's Roman Empire, nearly four millennia earlier. When power depends on "bread and circuses," those in power are compelled to provide ever greater largess if they wish to remain in power. To retain power, the political machines required an ever-filled public trough to buy off the Dolists, and the economy was crippled by inflation and debt. Even worse, with the network of tithes and transfer payments ensconced in the political will, graft and corruption had taken root and risen to full flower. It had become increasingly necessary for the political class (now incumbent sinecures in many cases) to support the lives to which they themselves had become accustomed. After almost two centuries of increasingly serious self-inflicted wounds and inflation, not even the once-robust Havenite economy could support that burden.

Even to the political ruling class, it was apparent that the entire socio-political edifice was in trouble: tax revenues had not matched expenditures in over 143 Standard years; R&D was faltering as an increasingly politicized (and hence ineffectual) educational system purveyed the pseudo-scientific mumbo-jumbo of collectivist economic theory rather than sound scientific training. On the manufacturing front, the decreasing numbers of truly capable industrial and technical managers produced by the system were finding it harder and harder to find positions where they could employ their skills and talents without having to pay bribes or curry political favor. Increasingly, these trained personnel were lured to other star systems whose economies allowed them to act on their abilities and enjoy the benefits thereof. In direct consequence, and after a lack of trained technicians resulted in a six month shortage of the Havenite electronics industry, the "Technical Conservation Act" of 1778 revoked emigration visas for all research and production engineers, nationalizing their expertise "as a resource of the Republic".

Real economic growth had lurched and halted in a cycle of recession and intervention to stave off depression; by the 1790s, economic growth by most conventional measures had stopped—indeed, the economy was contracting—and the stagflation which had resulted was becoming a self-sustaining reaction. In 1791 P.D., a highly classified economic report to the House of Legislators predicted that by the year 1850 the entire economy would collapse in a disaster which would make Old Earth's Great Depression and the Economic Winter of 252 P.D. look like mild recessions. The Chiefs of Staff, apprised of the degree of collapse to be anticipated, warned that it would precipitate pitched warfare in the streets as Haven's citizens fought for food for their families, for Haven had long since attained a population which could not feed itself without imports, and imports could not be paid for with a negative balance of trade.

The government saw only two ways out: to bite the bullet, end deficit spending, abolish the dole, and hope to weather the resultant catastrophic reorganization, or to find some other source of income to shore up the budget. The possibility of admitting they could no longer pay the interest on Haven's mortgaged future required a level of political courage bordering on suicide; while there were a few in the upper reaches of power in the House of Legislators with that much spine, there weren't enough of them to make a difference.

With no feasible way to survive owning up to the deficit spending, only the second solution was seriously considered. Regrettably, they had gone far on the right side of the Laffer curve, and there was no more money to be squeezed out of the economy. A panicked group of legislators suggested draconian "soak the rich" schemes, but the majority recognized that any such panacea would be purely cosmetic. Aside from their own hidden assets, the wealthy represented less than half of a percent of the total population, and the totally confiscatory taxes proposed would provide only a temporary reprieve. . . and eliminate both future private investment and the highest tax brackets (already taxed at 92% on personal income and 75% on investment income) as a long-term revenue source. A self-sustaining tax base could be produced only by a strong middle class, and the middle class had been systematically destroyed; what remained of it was far too small to sustain the government's current rate of expenditure and had been for over a century.

That left only one possible way to find the needed revenue, and the government, with the cooperation of the Quorum, prepared to seize it under the so-called "DuQuesne Plan".

THE DUQUESNE PLAN

The first step was a "Constitutional Convention" which radically rewrote the Haven Constitution. While maintaining a facade of democracy, the new constitution, by limiting eligibility requirements and office qualifications and giving the House of Legislators the right to refuse to seat even a legally elected representative if the House found him or her "personally unfit for public office," creating a legislative dictatorship with hereditary membership. (It was not a father-to-son inheritance but simply a codification of the "adoption" process which had become the normal career route for Havenite politicians over the past century; true dynasties came later.) The second step was not to limit deficit spending but to increase it, this time with the enthusiastic support of the military, which underwent the greatest peacetime expansion in Havenite history. The third step, launched in 1846 P.D., was to acquire new revenue from a totally new source: military conquest.

The initial attacks were practically unopposed. The sector was so accustomed to the idea that Haven represented the ideal to which all humanity aspired that its steady collapse under its own crushing weight of fiscal disaster had been grossly underestimated. While Haven's problems were known, the consensus was that all of them could be solved if Haven would only put its house in order; the true severity of Haven's financial crisis had been carefully withheld from its trading partners, to avoid deflating its bond rating.

Indeed, the majority of Haven's neighbors felt that the People's Republic was on the right track, but had simply gotten temporarily out of control. The fact that many of them were in the early stages of the same process in a sort of lemming-like emulation of disaster resulted in a set of political blinders of staggering proportions. The sudden expansion of the Havenite military caused some concern, but those who suggested that long-friendly Haven contemplated hostile action were viewed as hysterical alarmists. Besides, the sector's other systems found their own economies were becoming increasingly strapped, and warships and troops cost money which was required for their own welfare programs.

The result was a turkey shoot for the Peoples' Navy. Between 1846 and 1900 P.D., barely half a century, the People's Republic of Haven had conquered every inhabited star system within a hundred light years of it, incorporating them by force into a new, interstellar People's Republic of Haven ruled by the now openly hereditary "House of Legislators" of the Haven System.

Unfortunately for the House of Legislators, conquest was not the panacea they had hoped. True, they could loot the economies of conquered worlds, but unless they wanted servile insurrection, there was a limit to how badly they could wreck their subject economies…and the subject economies, once crushed, produced additional burdens. Worse, the military machine required to conquer and then police their new empire cost even more than they had anticipated, particularly as their alarmed and (so far) unconquered neighbors began to arm in reply. Despite all efforts, their budgets remained stubbornly in the deficit column; they simply could not pay for both their military and the support of their subsidized population out of available resources. There was an appearance of prosperity on the home front, but those in informed positions knew that it was only an appearance. In short, the "Republic" had only two options: continue to expand, or collapse.

THE HAVEN-MANTICORE WAR

The Havenite Expansion, or, more properly, the DuQuesne Plan, requires the acquisition of subordinate economies to be integrated into the People's Republic. Indeed, poor selection of targets in the decades leading up to the 20th century P.D. has caused problems for the People's Republic akin to indigestion – they ultimately cost more than they had added to the coffers. This required an adjustment of priorities, including taking on objectives with higher military risk for greater potential reward. Most notably, this meant engagement with the Star Kingdom of Manticore.

One of the principal reasons for conquering the Star Kingdom of Manticore is its six-terminus wormhole junction; with this under Havenite control, the routes for future expansion, or even taking revenue for transit fees, could sustain the People's Republic for decades, if not centuries. It also stood to reason that the People's Navy could take the Manticore Binary System if it could force enough ships through the out-system termini. Of the termini available, Trevor's Star was already in Havenite hands, Gregor ran the risk of engaging the Andermani Empire, and Beowulf required carving through the massive Solarian League. Of the other three, two lay so far away from the Republic that sending expeditionary forces to capture them were military suicide. Basilisk was held by the Star Kingdom directly, but on a protectorate basis, and was not particularly fortified. While mounting a full-on invasion of Basilisk would be expensive, the Havenite assessment of the internal Manticoran political environment held out a prospect of capturing it short of all out war.

Operation Odysseus

The objective of Odysseus was to take the Basilisk system, giving a second avenue for an assault on Manticore. Optimally, Haven would declare sovereignty over the system without engaging in outright hostilities with the Star Kingdom, giving it time to build a strike force and place it there, with a second at Trevor's Star.

Odysseus hinged upon legalisms in the original Manticoran act of annexation. Due to the political battle in the House of Lords, the Star Kingdom specifically denied perpetual sovereignty over the planet of Medusa, establishing it as a native protectorate to be released to the natives "at the earliest possible convenience." Between that, a conservative First Lord of the Admiralty, and general lack of activity in the system, Basilisk's forces had been gradually drawn down for actions in Silesia or elsewhere, leaving just a handful of screening units.

The first order of Odysseus was to create a native Medusan insurrection, using the slaughter of off-worlders as a pretext for intervention by a Havenite task force. Once the situation planetside stabilized, the task force commander would proclaim Haven's possession of the system, as Manticore had demonstrated its inability to maintain order and public safety on the planet's surface.

Regrettably, the timing of Odysseus involved a change of command on Basilisk station; Captain Pavel Young's replacement, Commander Honor Harrington, worked more closely with Medusan personnel, and managed to get better cooperation from the Native Protection Agency. This, and a very risky intervention with her Marine complement allowed the native insurrection to be suppressed before it reached the human inhabited areas of the

planet. When the planetside part of the operation was falling to pieces, both the Havenite embassy's courier boat and the armed merchant cruiser PNSS *Sirius* broke orbit to tell the task force to stand down. After disabling the courier boat's impeller nodes with a risky close range pass, HMS *Fearless* gave chase to the *Sirius*. In a running battle that stretched across the system, *Fearless* destroyed the *Sirius* at tremendous loss of life. Despite being tried in absentia and found guilty of piracy and murder by a Havenite court, Commander Harrington was awarded a commendation and promotion for her actions in Basilisk.

The fallout from the Basilisk Incident was severe. By Crown Proclamation, any Haven-registered ship passing through the Junction, regardless of destination or normal diplomatic immunity, was forced submit to boarding and search before she would be allowed passage. Moreover, no Havenite warship was permitted transit under any circumstances. The incident also gave the Crown adequate justification to accelerate its naval construction program.

The People's Navy grossly underestimated the capabilities of the Star Kingdom's new construction, with a mindset still blinded by its tonnage and overall materiel advantages. Manticore's Foreign Office also succeeded in coaxing the Solarian League to embargo sales of military technology to both sides. This embargo, while damaging to several Solarian interests, seems to have favored the Star Kingdom considerably.

The collapse of Operation Odysseus set back the Havenite timetables by at least two years. The change in operational tempo, and the creation of a larger picket force at the Basilisk terminus, meant that a direct grab there had moved past the threshold of acceptable risk for the People's Navy, due to the logistical constraints imposed by digesting their latest conquests. The Manticoran advantage of interior lines as well as the ability to use the Manticore Wormhole Junction to move forces from different termini to the home system as reinforcements, meant that a single pronged assault from Trevor's Star meant that a defeat in detail was likely. A new plan of attack would be needed.

Operation Jericho

Following the Basilisk Incident, both the Star Kingdom of Manticore and People's Republic of Haven knew a full scale conflict was coming. Over the next eighteen months, the People's Navy moved to take several systems to serve as forward bases against Manticore. In response, the Star Kingdom began a diplomatic offensive to build an alliance of single system polities, asking for basing rights, and transferring construction of lighter units to their shipyards.

Both sides saw the Yeltsin's Star system as a thin point on the Manticoran frontier. The Manticoran government was actively courting the Protectorate of Grayson, looking for basing rights in return for technology transfers. In response, the People's Republic "sold" two modern Havenite warships to Masada, providing training and trained personnel to operate them.

Shortly after the convoy bearing Manticoran diplomatic personnel arrived in the Yeltsin's Star system, the Masadan Navy launched a devastating attack. Nearly the entire Grayson Space Navy, along with one Manticoran destroyer, were eliminated by the Masadan forces, acting in concert with their newly acquired Havenite warships. Further, Masada's agents within the Grayson government attempted to assassinate Benjamin Mayhew, putting his cousing Jared in the Protectorship. Quick intervention by RMN personnel foiled the coup attempt, though not without a great loss of life. With the failure of the coup, aggressive investigation of the local Masadan intelligence network pinpointed a supply and logistics node at Blackbird in the outer system of Yeltsin's Star. Because of the direct (and publicly broadcast) heroism shown by the Manticoran personnel, the Havenite commander of MNS *Thunder of God* declared the political aspect of the operation to be a failure, as no military action on his part could conceivably force the Graysons and Manticorans apart. His Masadan crew mutinied, and took *Thunder of God* on a mission to rain destruction on Grayson. Two Manticoran ships, the HMS *Fearless* and HMS *Troubadour* fought a desperate delaying action against the *Thunder of God*, with the loss of the destroyer. The commander of the *Fearless*, coincidentally the commander on the spot at Basilisk, managed to survive by dint of a near-miraculous intervention of Admiral White Haven. She earned the Star of Grayson, and a fair amount of political clout on Grayson, and by doing so, has come to represent the personal embodiment of the Grayson/Manticoran alliance.

As the result of the very visible price Manticore was willing to pay to defend its allies, the ultimate result of the Battles of Yeltsin's Star were far greater than their military potential indicates; the following 14 months allowed Manticore to woo several new systems into its alliance, citing the actions of Grayson as an indicator of their level of commitment. This greatly expanded the strategic reach of the Royal Manticoran Navy, through a network of interlocking supply and maintenance bases along the frontier.

While the Alliance was expanding, the People's Republic's efforts went into securing a number of systems in strategic positions relative to Alliance territory, including upgrading them to forward supply bases for Operation Perseus.

Operation Argus
Shortly after the technology embargo was put into place and tested diplomatically, the People's Navy implemented Operation Argus. Argus used drone chassis procured clandestinely from rogue League arms dealers. These stealthy, high endurance observation drones were inserted from well outside standard sensor range. Low powered, they were designed to accelerate and decelerate into positions around the system ecliptic, to observe traffic patterns and deduce Manticoran operational deployments. With the gradual formation of the Manticoran Alliance, Haven seems to have deployed Argus sensors as fast as the Alliance terms were agreed to, and data was collected and tabulated for two standard years, laying the groundwork for other, more direct operations.

Operation Perseus
Operation Perseus was the first strike into Manticoran territory. Using an increasingly heavy series of raids and diversionary attacks on Alliance systems to draw the Royal Manticoran Navy into strategic dispersal, Perseus sought to undermine the stability of the Alliance. As the dominant military member, Manticore's credibility was built on their ability to protect fellow Alliance members, Perseus was designed to present the RMN with overwhelming and widespread commitments that could not be abandoned politically. The truism of "He who attempts to protect everything defends nothing" is as applicable in modern Naval operations as it was to Sun Tzu 6,000 years ago.

Phase one of Operation Perseus was a series of minor provocations. These included violations of Alliance territory and attacks on convoys in Alliance space. Similar attacks on convoys occurred at Ramon, Quentin, Clearaway and Yeltsin. In each case, either Manticore or her allies lost shipping and lives. The Yeltsin attack was the most severe, destroying all three merchants and their escorts. Other attacks hit Candor, Klein Station and Zuckerman.

The RMN's response was to strengthen escorting forces, and shift deployments to counter threats to allied systems. Even so, this left thin spots in patrol coverage. The Havenites, armed with data from Argus, capitalized on this, dispatching forces to attack patrols in Poicters, Talbot, Mendoza and Zanzibar. In each case, the Havenites sent sufficient forces to guarantee the destruction of their objectives. Strategically, the Havenites had taken control of the tempo of the war, though at a higher cost than had been anticipated, though still within "budget". Outside observers have used the loss rates from the Havenite forces to assess the Manticoran electronics systems as being comparable to the Solarian League's, or at worst, only slightly inferior. After the attacks and follow on raids, Manticore stopped short of a formal declaration of war, but closed the Manticore Wormhole Junction to Havenite shipping and ejected all diplomatic courier boats from Alliance space. The RMN also began shadowing and harassing Havenite convoys moving through Alliance territory.

While certain that the Havenites were due to lay down a hammer blow of an attack, the RMN had no idea where it would come from. Furthermore, unaware of the Argus probes, the RMN took the lack of obvious intelligence gathering methods—typically done with scout destroyers cutting across the outer edge of a system to gather impeller signature data—as a sign that the Havenites were slowing their operational tempo down. With no Havenite scouting pickets detected, and with a broad zone of commitments to cover, the commander of Hancock station dispersed his forces to protect Zanzibar, Alizon and Yorik. When the Havenites received the Argus data for this series of departures, they moved to take Hancock, hoping to destroy the repair base. While Hancock was being attacked, another attempt at the Yeltsin system was also unleashed.

Battle of Hancock
The Battle of Hancock was, for the People's Navy, proof that letting commanders have individual discretion is the route to disaster. While attempting to attain local superiority in multiple places, the initial assault on Hancock was whittled down to less than half by the defenders; when Manticoran reinforcements arrived, they arrived before the Havenite reinforcements did. Furthermore, when Manticoran fleet elements were pulled from other systems, they also raided Seaford system, destroying the Havenite repair base there, and forcing most of the People's Navy's operational staff back to Barnett.

Third Battle of Yeltsin
The People's Navy went into Yeltsin believing they had a three-to-one advantage, only to find himself facing a force even stronger their own; using techniques that can only be described as miraculous luck, the Manticorans had managed to position an ambush force in-system. A quarter of the Havenite fleet was rendered inoperable in the opening salvoes, and after-action reports show that the Manticoran pod launching system was instrumental in creating this casualty rate. The Havenite task force fought clear of Yeltsin with barely half the ships that had entered it, and half of them had been so battered their return to Barnett had taken more than twice as long as the passage out.

STARSHIP TACTICS

The People's Navy has the leading edge in practical combat experience with impeller drive missiles, including the doctrinal adjustments forced by laser warheads. Laser heads, and the means to produce them, were acquired from the Solarian League in the 1880s. Ostensibly, the Solarian League sale was meant to recoup the investment in the technology after the bid failed to meet with SLN approvals; other sources indicate that the initial set were provided to the Havenite Navy along with observers.

The advent of the laser head forced a change in defensive doctrines for ships. First, due to the detonation rage being at ~30,000 km, rather than trying to reach the sidewall directly, they demanded a shift from point defense cluster suites to countermissiles, though point defense clusters remain an important "second chance" defensive layer. Secondarily, laser heads, while not as devastating per hit as a contact nuke could be, were much less of an "all or nothing" sort of attack. A ship killed by laser heads could be described as "death by a thousand pinpricks". The third doctrinal shift in laser heads was a reduction of the utility of rolling wedge. A laser head is capable of drifting over the edge an interposed wedge and firing "down" into the sidewall of the ship. This doesn't render rolling wedge useless, but does mitigate it considerably. This, in conjunction with how damage resolves against the hull of the ship (single medium to deep strikes against the superstructure, rather than scouring the surface off with a contact nuke) resulted in the missile battle becoming more decisive.

The People's Navy's experience during the DuQuesne expansion resulted in several refits, and a gradual escalation of tonnage in a given "range" of ships, with one of the more exaggerated cases being the *Mars-A* and *Mars-B* class cruisers.

In terms of doctrinal fighting, the optimum case is to have your force's broadside bearing down the unprotected throat or kilt of your target's impeller wedge. Achieving this in a vector movement environment is far from elementary, and requires some aspects of cooperation from the enemy, usually as they change their heading in preparation to accelerate for a different bearing.

As relying on the enemy cooperating with your plans isn't a recipe for success, the most common case is a broadside-on-broadside duel with missiles, typically starting at under 20 light seconds, with a closing vector on the target. If you can pin the target against an objective, the attacker can define how close the closest approach will be; ranges of under two light seconds put you into beam engagement ranges, where the battles become short, brutal and decisive.

Defending against the broadside duel is as simple as rolling 90 degrees, and bringing the gravity bands of the impeller between you and the target. This significantly degrades sensor performance, and removes your own offensive weapons and countermissiles from the equation. Against contact nuclear warheads, rolling the wedge was a near perfect defense; with the advent of laser heads, point defense clusters have been reprogrammed to take snap shots against warheads clearing the wedge before they can fire into the sidewall of the ship. Most approaches would have screening units facing the enemy, relaying telemetry data to the main force, which

is rolled wedge-on to preserve combat capabilities until the range is decisive enough to fire.

For battles that are larger than the single ship duel, or small squadron action, the permutations of doctrine vary from navy to navy, while remaining within the parameters set by the physics of the technology. Warships have extensive sensor arrays for coordinating offensive and countermissile fire, and there are significant advantages in doing so – attempting to generate an overwhelming throw weight of missiles at a target downrange, or protecting one target in the core of a formation with massed countermissile fire. Stacking units vertically as well as horizontally, in a line one ship thick is known as the Wall of Battle. It effectively spreads the formation along both axes perpendicular to the objective, allowing a fleet to coordinate its fire to maximum density. The Wall of Battle is a standard part of most naval doctrines, though it is cumbersome in deployment, requiring a near iron-clad adherence to maneuver control on evolutions and positional changes within the formation to avoid hazarding other ships with wedge interference or, worse yet, entanglement.

In tactical deployment, the "face" of the wall is arrayed tangentially to the unit's vector closing on the objective, with screening elements placed such that their vectors will let them drift "behind" the wall of battle before they get picked off by overwhelming firepower. This waltz of vectors requires years of training to execute properly. When a wall of battle is outmatched, the standard counter is to have each unit of the wall roll wedge to the enemy to cover themselves for a retreat, while accelerating for a retreat. The rolled force has the option of rolling back in most cases if the enemy turns throat-on to them to close the vectors, though most enemies aren't so obliging, aiming to cause a vector intercept at a defined point in the future set by relative acceleration abilities.

WEDGE FIELD DIAGRAM

Dorsal Wedge

Ship (not to scale)

Forward View

Ventral Wedge

Forward and aft impeller rings work in tandem to create the drive field.

THE WALL OF BATTLE

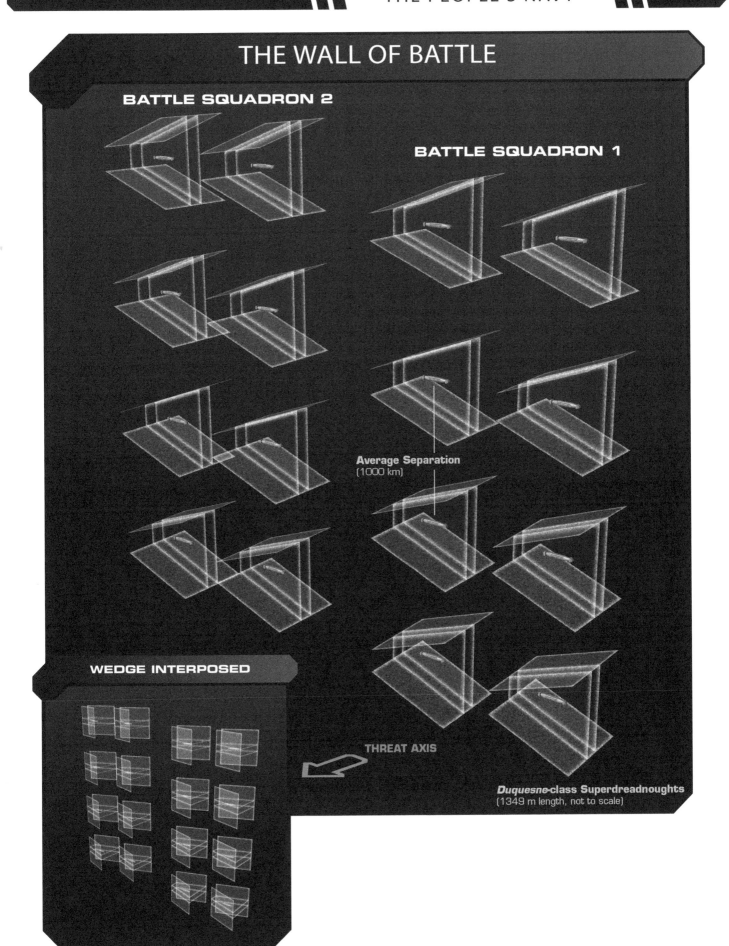

BATTLE SQUADRON 2

BATTLE SQUADRON 1

Average Separation
(1000 km)

WEDGE INTERPOSED

THREAT AXIS

Duquesne-class Superdreadnoughts
(1349 m length, not to scale)

THE PEOPLE'S NAVY

The People's Navy uses the squadron as both an administrative unit and for tactical coordination. This follows modern practice inherited from the Solarian League. The People's Navy is fairly rigid about organization, with even smaller ships closely coordinated at an administrative and tactical level.

Battlecruisers are tightly integrated into the wall of battle, and organized into 8-ship squadrons accordingly. Heavy cruisers are organized into similarly sized squadrons as part of the screen. Recently, the People's Navy has been experimenting with 6-ship "short" squadrons of heavy cruisers for commerce and infrastructure raiding.

Officially there is only one Fleet in the People's Navy, most operational level organization uses Task Forces and Task Groups split off from the main fleet. This has served them well in their initial conquests, where their operational pattern was to deploy the number of ships necessary to secure the target, then bring the bulk of the Task Force back after the system was pacified, leaving only a small Task Group for orbital security.

As the true scope of a multi-system war sets in, it is only a matter of time before the People's Navy subdivides into fully independent fleets.

TACTICAL ORGANIZATION

Formation	Abbrev	Composition
Destroyer Division	DesDiv	4 DD
Destroyer Squadron	DesRon	3 DesDiv (12 DD)
Destroyer Flotilla	DesFlot	2 DesRon (24 DD)
Light Cruiser Division	CruDiv	4 CL
Light Cruiser Squadron	CruRon	3 CruDiv (12 CL)
Heavy Cruiser Division	CruDiv	2 CA
Heavy Cruiser Squadron	CruRon	4 CruDiv (8 CA)
Battlecruiser Division	BatCruDiv	2 BC
Battlecruiser Squadron	BatCruRon	4 BatCruDiv (8 BC)
Battle Division	BatDiv	2 BB, DN, SD
Battle Squadron	BatRon	4 BatDiv (8 BB, DN, SD)
Task Group	TG	(varies)
Task Force	TF	(varies)
Fleet		(varies)

ADMINISTRATIVE ORGANIZATION

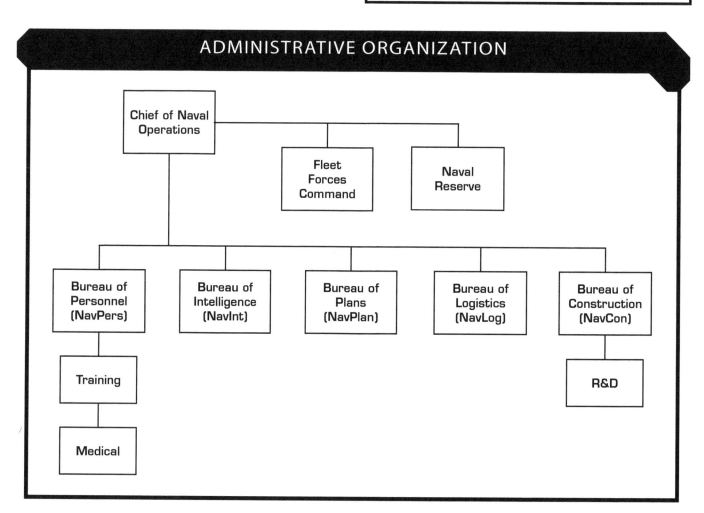

TASK FORCE 21 IN ACTION

OFFICER CORPS AND RANK STRUCTURE

The People's Navy officer corps is comprised of long-term volunteer professionals. Organizationally, it demands officers who go by the book. While the RMN may tolerate loose cannons such as Harrington and White Haven, the need to keep systems pacified, with a quick reaction force on hand to carry out solid, confirmed doctrine in concordance with the People's Republic's political will makes this unacceptable. The People's Navy expects its officers to accept their orders, confirm receipt within the chain of command, do as they are told, and report the results, with the results showing conformity with standard doctrine.

While that structure of centralized control is the ideal that the People's Navy aspires to, the expanse of the People's Republic makes it impractical. With no instantaneous communications, commanders can and do get put into places where they have to go "beyond the book". If their decisions are sanctioned by their superiors after the fact, then their career is made, while any failure will fall squarely on their own shoulders. The People's Navy considers this to be part and parcel of the burden of command, though it results in "careerism" and taking the safest choice regardless of the situation. A Havenite officer dares not deviate (openly, at least) from the "party line". Few officers not sponsored by a Legislaturalist family reach flag rank, and only members of those families ever pass the rank of rear admiral.

The bulk of Havenite enlisted personnel are conscripts; current estimates are upwards of seventy percent as of this writing. While some media members have portrayed this as the equivalent of "impressing" sailors on the high seas, with horrific morale and abuses, the reality is far cleaner than that. For many Dolists, conscription is seen, not as a way of doing one's duty to the People's Republic, but simply a case of bad luck, much like drawing a jail sentence might be—and, like time spent in a prison, time spent in the Navy offers valuable skills when you get out. Significantly, the retention rate for conscripts after their initial

5 Haven year enlistment hovers right around 40%. Apparently, once the adjustment to military life is made, it is often preferable to living in a Dolist project. The PN's petty officers, the backbone of any navy, average less than a dozen years in grade; because the turnover in conscript crews means that it's harder to cultivate competent subordinates, but mostly it comes from the realization that, having made it as a petty officer in the PN, one's prospects in the civilian job market – even one as wretched as Haven's, represent a significant boost in quality of life.

A very few People's Navy enlisted personnel enter OCS; surprisingly, most of those that do are Junior Petty Officers. A large cadre of the officers will deem a mustang to be their social and intellectual inferior. Given the product of Haven's schools, this is not an unwarranted assumption. Meanwhile, the enlisted the officer is supervising, once they discover he was once "one of them", turn their general apathy towards officers into an active hostility for the person who "betrayed his people" to become one.

The progressive "democratization" of the People's Republic's education system has ruined instruction for subjects requiring mathematical skills or "trade" skills. The best-educated enlisted personnel of the People's Navy are conscripts from recently conquered planets. As a consequence of this educational malaise, the People's Republic has a different attitude towards many shipboard practices. Among them is that damage control should be "black boxed." A component that fails a test is pulled from service and replaced with a spare, and is repaired at base or discarded. The People's Navy spends significant sums on caches of spare parts, due to this lack of onboard parts repair capability. This influences ship construction techniques, forcing standardized parts for use across multiple classes of ships. This practice has slowed the pace of innovation in the People's Navy's ship construction, as ship designers have learned they'll have to fight dearly for every new or non-standard part in the Navy.

OFFICER'S UNDRESS UNIFORM

The People's Navy officer's undress uniform consists of a short, forest green jacket, a white blouse and grey trousers.

The jacket design is similar to something called an "Ike Jacket" for reasons lost to history. It has pockets to either side of the midline seal, double pointed collars and an integral belt at the waist. Aside from the lower forearm, which is black to set off the cuff rings, the jacket is untrimmed.

The blouse is white with a wraparound turtleneck collar that seals with a flap on the left. The shoulders carry rank insignia on flexible "shoulder boards" that fit comfortably under the jacket.

The trousers are loose and straight cut down to cover the tops of the boots. A black belt with silver buckle is partly hidden by the jacket. Piping up the sides is color coded to department.

Cuff rings are gold braid on a black background. The topmost ring breaks to a loop in the center, with half rings to indicate junior ranks and double rings to indicate flag ranks. Matching stripes are carried on the jacket's shoulder boards and those of the blouse.

Collar insignia is worn on the lower points of the jacket and consists of a "train track" of interconnected gold bars. Silver bars are used for junior ranks and double wide bars for flag ranks.

Ribbons are worn just above the pocket on the left side, immediately to the right of the symbol of The People's Republic. The exception is the Order of Valor, which is always worn on the right side.

Line officers wear a peaked green cap with a black visor and the symbol of the People's Republic embroidered on the front. Flag officers replace the embroidery with a gold and silver pin.

OFFICER'S UNIFORM AND SKINSUIT

UNDRESS UNIFORM

SKINSUIT

DEPARTMENTS

- COMMAND / FLAG
- ADMINISTRATIVE
- TACTICAL
- ENGINEERING
- ASTROGATION
- COMMUNICATIONS
- LOGISTICS
- MEDICAL

ARMED FORCES PIN

INSIGNIA

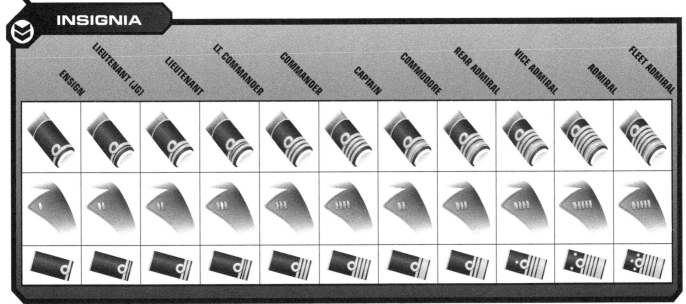

ENSIGN · LIEUTENANT (JG) · LIEUTENANT · LT. COMMANDER · COMMANDER · CAPTAIN · COMMODORE · REAR ADMIRAL · VICE ADMIRAL · ADMIRAL · FLEET ADMIRAL

ENLISTED UNDRESS UNIFORM

The enlisted undress uniform consists of a one-piece grey coverall, belted at the waist, made of a poly-cotton blend. The fit is considerably looser than the officer's uniform. It's designed to be practical, functional gear, though the process of using a head causes many to grumble incessantly about the "one piece" nature of the garment, particularly among female personnel. It has two pockets on the chest, and two cargo pockets on the legs, plus stylus holding loops in the cuffs. The coverall seals up the front to an open collar, and the collar has sensors that record pulse rate and respiration rates so personnel can be monitored for overwork or dehydration.

The garments are color coded by department, with the colored panels on the top two thirds of the left side chest, over the shoulder and down one third of the back. This makes it easier for new officers to identify which enlisted personnel are "theirs" and makes it easier for a new recruit to find his workmates for on the job training.

Spacer identification is shown by a nametag, worn over the left breast pocket; the left edge of the nametag has a series of pips for service awards. A silver pip is awarded for five Havenite years (almost six T-years) of service while a gold pip is awarded for every ten years of service. All name tags are encoded with radio frequency IDs, which allow tracking of personnel to the compartment level throughout the ship; this feature has resulted in a minor black market of "false ID" tags, usually sold to enlisted personnel who need to "be in two places at once" for functions both official and unsanctioned. While the People's Navy has advocated more reliance on the nametags and their RFID bugs, experienced NCOs quickly develop an instinct for detecting such chicanery.

An enlisted man's rating insignia is color coded to match his department, like the chest panel. It is worn on the upper left sleeve, and specialty insignia for petty officers and warrant officers are worn above the rating insignia.

The enlisted cap is standard navy grey with a black band. The cap is soft peaked at the front and back and untrimmed.

Even with rapid promotions, there are few senior petty officers and fewer chief petty officers in the People's Navy. Many positions that would normally be filled by a petty officer are filled by a commissioned officer instead.

While press coverage of Havenite fashion trends is minimal, snide commentary has been made of the similarity in cut between the Havenite enlisted uniform, and the standard garments issued to Dolist workers and medium security inmates in the Republic.

SKINSUIT

The skinsuits worn by the People's Navy are typical of the tech base that produced them. They are bulky and utilitarian. While they lack several sophisticated features, they are functional and considerably less expensive than their Manticoran counterparts.

The storage vacuoles used are several generations behind those used in most modern skinsuits, which adds to the bulk of the body suit and reduces their endurance to only 6 hours. On the other hand, they are considerably lighter, and require a lesser degree of augmentation to maneuver comfortably, and they are significantly easier to manufacture and keep maintained, particularly given the limited technical manpower of the People's Navy. The PRH's skinsuit is one of its primary technological exports to outlying star systems. While the Manticoran design is inarguably superior in every technical aspect, the Havenite design is less expensive (especially when factoring in economies of scale) and cheaper to maintain and operate.

The suit's standard medical panel is hidden behind a press-seal flap on the chest. Stimulants and painkillers can be dispensed with a single keypress. The emergency tourniquet system is also controlled from the medical panel.

The keypad on the left arm (right arm for left handed crewmen) is uncovered, but can be locked to prevent accidental keypresses. Most suit functions are controlled from this keypad, which includes a small readout to display suit integrity status.

The suit's umbilical attachment is on the front slightly off the left hip. This puts it just below the normal range of movement for the left arm while seated, while still allowing a firm connection.

The helmet design is less bulky than the RMN helmet, but has a much narrower field of view. The People's Navy does not require headgear to be worn under the helmet. In-helmet controls and the head's up display are similar to the Manticoran design.

The thrusters are designed for emergency use only, with an endurance of only a few minutes of sustained thrust. This is sufficient for emergency egress from a damaged ship, but for extended EVA work, small maneuvering sleds or strap-on thruster units are used.

Both officers and enlisted skinsuits are white, trimmed over the shoulders and down the inside of the arms with reflective striping color coded by department. While the helmets have traditionally been white, a recent redesign introduced the black helmets shown here.

Officers' suits display rank stripes on the cuffs much like the undress uniform tunic. Officer's skinsuits may come with or without cargo pockets on the legs, a decision that is usually left up to individual preference.

ENLISTED UNIFORM AND SKINSUIT

UNDRESS UNIFORM

SKINSUIT

NAMETAG

DREHLER

CONTROL PANEL

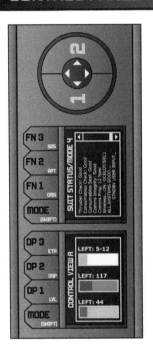

INSIGNIA

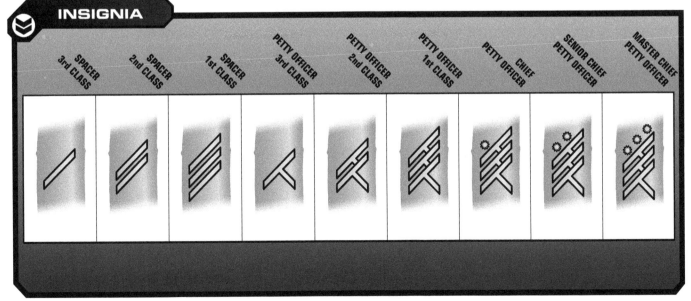

SPACER 3rd CLASS

SPACER 2nd CLASS

SPACER 1st CLASS

PETTY OFFICER 3rd CLASS

PETTY OFFICER 2nd CLASS

PETTY OFFICER 1st CLASS

CHIEF PETTY OFFICER

SENIOR CHIEF PETTY OFFICER

MASTER CHIEF PETTY OFFICER

SHIPS OF THE PEOPLE'S NAVY

Warships in the People's Navy are, as a rule, built tough and dependable. Their design philosophy could easy be summed up with the simple statement "better is the enemy of good enough."

Whenever possible, complex systems are replaced by simpler systems. A notable example of this is in the passive defenses. A Havenite warship has weaker sidewalls, but comparatively heavier armor than a Manticoran or Solarian. This fits Havenite centralized planning and logistical doctrine - armor plating requires less maintenance man-hours than sidewall generators do.

Weapon mounts are clustered by type to simplify power requirements, control runs and ammunition handling. With neighboring mounts often sharing critical power and control subsystems, chances increase that a single hit can take out multiple weapons of the same type. Havenite warships have fewer, larger magazines shared by multiple launchers, rather than compartmentalizing launchers and magazines into smaller units.

Havenite warships spend long spans between scheduled maintenance runs. Given the lower standards of training and education that the People's Navy must accept, their crews are poorly suited to many routine maintenance tasks. Most of their electronic equipment is built to a profoundly modular standard, where full modules are pulled and replaced without any attempt to repair them in-place. Anything more complex is left for the support ships or forward repair bases. This puts a premium on the shipboard diagnostic systems, and the People's Navy leads the militaries of known space in this aspect of the electronics field.

Every ship has a sophisticated expert system installed to diagnose maintenance issues and suggest courses of action to the engineering department. For simple swap-and-replace level fixes, the system can quickly find the faulty component, and every system has built-in threshold monitoring to flag faults that must be repaired at a yard. If such a condition exists, the system reports to

the Chief Engineer, who reports to the captain, who then informs the squadron CO and departs for the nearest repair base.

When a ship returns from a deployment period, scheduled or unscheduled, the crew departs and the shipyard technicians take over. The yard workers are among the most highly trained technical staff in the People's Navy, and there are substantial retention bonuses to keep them in uniform. Where other navies treat yard dogs as "those who couldn't quite cut it to be senior engineering staff on a mobile command", the People's Navy, short on qualified technical personnel, husbands them as a critical, centralized resource. There is almost no contact between the yard workers and the ship's crew, including the engineering staff. Maintenance reports, both human and ship-generated, are reviewed by the yard workers, who perform the necessary maintenance and repairs.

This system has greatly simplified the logistics tail for a given operation, reduced reliance on variable quality engineering crews and ensured a high percentage of uptime for their warships. The drawbacks include ships that are optimized more for the convenience of the yard workers than damage control teams. Heavy armor around critical combat systems can be bypassed by the yard tech teams, but does not provide easy access during a combat situation.

The start of the Manticore War pointed out a greater flaw in the system. Prior to the war, all conquests were quick single-system affairs. Fleet organization was tightly centralized, and other than convoy escorts, few ships operated far from their bases for extended periods of time. A multi-system war has heavily taxed the ability of the Office of Naval Logistics to keep pace with warship deployments. Even with a higher percentage of forward nodal bases than the Manticoran Alliance, the People's Navy is seeing widespread declines in efficiency and readiness reports as ships are forced to spend more time on deployment.

SIZE COMPARISON

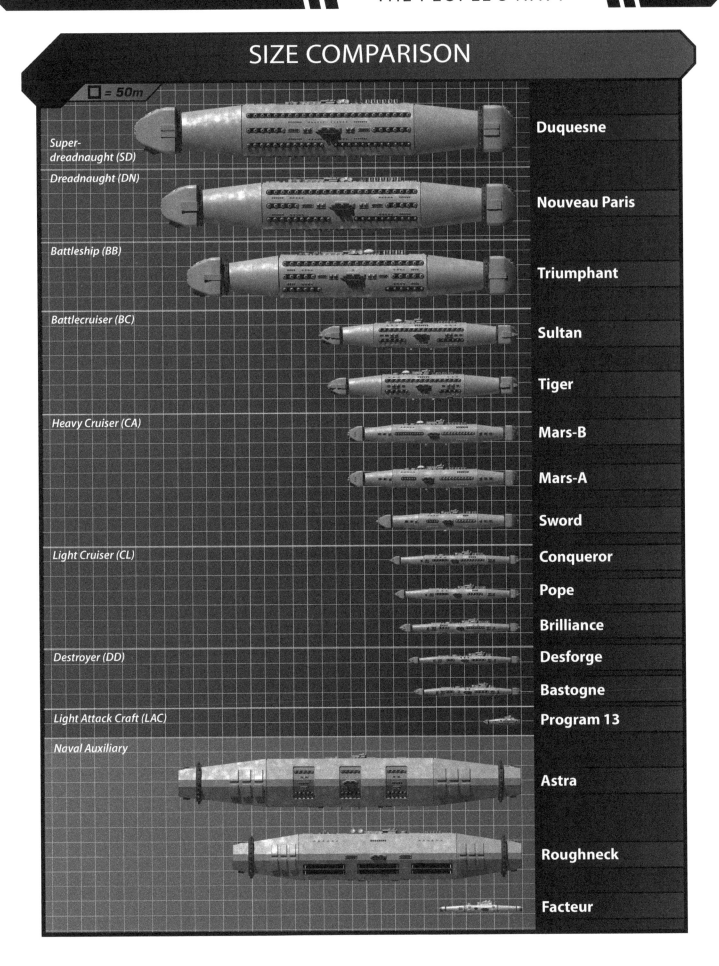

□ = 50m

Super-dreadnaught (SD)	Duquesne
Dreadnaught (DN)	Nouveau Paris
Battleship (BB)	Triumphant
Battlecruiser (BC)	Sultan
	Tiger
Heavy Cruiser (CA)	Mars-B
	Mars-A
	Sword
Light Cruiser (CL)	Conqueror
	Pope
	Brilliance
Destroyer (DD)	Desforge
	Bastogne
Light Attack Craft (LAC)	Program 13
Naval Auxiliary	Astra
	Roughneck
	Facteur

DUQUESNE-CLASS SUPERDREADNOUGHT

Ships in Class
D'Allonville, Alphand, Baudin, Charette, Duquesne, Forbin, Guichen, D'Iberville, Lepanto, Mouchez, Tilden, Rousseau, Salamis

Estimated Service Dates
1879 to 1948 PD

Specification
Mass: 7,939,250 tons
Length: 1,349 m
Beam: 196 m
Draught: 182 m
Acceleration: 407.5 G
Crew: 4790 (626 Officers, 3550 Enlisted, 614 Marines)
Power:
 5 RF/9 Golfech 3 Fusion Reactors
Electronics
 AG-2(a) Gravitic Detection Array
 AR-2 Phased Radar Array
 AL-3 Lidar Array
 SLCF-17 116x104-channel Distributed Control System
 ARBB-16 Electronic Countermeasures
Armament:
 92 LM-8 Capital Ship Missile Tubes
 8 L/300 Capital Ship Lasers
 12 G/398 Grasers
 24 L/280 Capital Ship Lasers
 24 G/357 Grasers
 80 LMC-8(c) Counter Missile Tubes
 72 P/16x8 Anti-Missile Lasers
Magazines
 11412 L13(a) Capital Ship Missiles
 24080 C2 Counter Missiles
 20 LAD-5 Tethered ECM Decoys
Small Craft:
 8 DB.100 *Mercure*-class Cutters
 6 D.435 *Ouragan*-class Pinnaces

Design and Construction
The *DuQuesne*-class superdreadnought, at 7.9 million tons, is one of the largest of the modern People's Navy superdreadnought classes. It is, counting all of its variants, the most numerous superdreadnought class in the Havenite inventory. In terms of design, the *DuQuesne* is a conservative class, with a conventional mix of missile tubes, beam weapons, active defenses and armor. The class's immediate lineage can be traced back to one of the earliest Havenite dreadnought classes, the *Hempstead*, and shows a mild break from the "win the engagement in the first salvo" doctrine with the wall of battle ships.

The current flight of the *DuQuesne* is the Flight V. The change from Flight I to Flight II improved the sidewall strength and hammerhead armor. Going from Flight II to Flight III replaced a quarter of the broadside point defense clusters with countermissile tubes, upgrading from the AR-2 Phased Radar array to the more capable AR-7(b) system. Flight IV re-arranged a number of the interior spaces for ease of maintenance, while improving the sidewalls a second time, and Flight V added 3 salvoes of magazine

stowage to each broadside through use of an improved feed mechanism.

Particularly after the Flight IV revision, the *DuQuesne* is one of the most comfortable and sought after command and flag billets in the People's Navy. Because of the thought put into the design for future expansion, and the attendant space made for storage of spare parts, and sensibly arranged accessways, the *DuQuesne* has one of the best per-class rates of uptime and readiness of any ship type in the People's Navy. The *DuQuesne* class incorporates several lessons learned from decades of military expansion, including a heaver allotment of active defenses, and operations research derived models of optimum compartment armoring.

There is a design study in the works for a 44-tube broadside replacement for the *DuQuesne*; it has not gotten much political traction, as the People's Navy is reluctant to change superdreadnought designs from something that works to something that reflects doctrinal purity at a likely cost in uptime.

Doctrinal Notes
The *DuQuesne*-class is a standard "ship of the wall"; it has an extensive broadside of capital missiles, and the lasers and grasers to end battles decisively once it reaches beam range. In deployment, it gets used in full superdreadnought divisions and squadrons, rather than being penny parceled out.

Notable Units and Engagements
The first ship of this class, PNS *DuQuesne*, was commissioned and put to its first space trials prematurely, when Anton DuQuesne, the political heir of the architect of the DuQuesne plan, died in an aircar accident. Named in his honor, and commissioned as a monument to the architect of the vision of Havenite expansion, the first *DuQuesne* had more than its fair share of working up trials, and many faults attributed to its rapid completion. As a result, it was permanently attached to Home Fleet, where it serves as a training facility. Further ships of the class have served up and down the Manticoran front, but no single unit has achieved any distinction at this time.

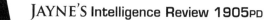

DUQUESNE - TECHNICAL READOUT

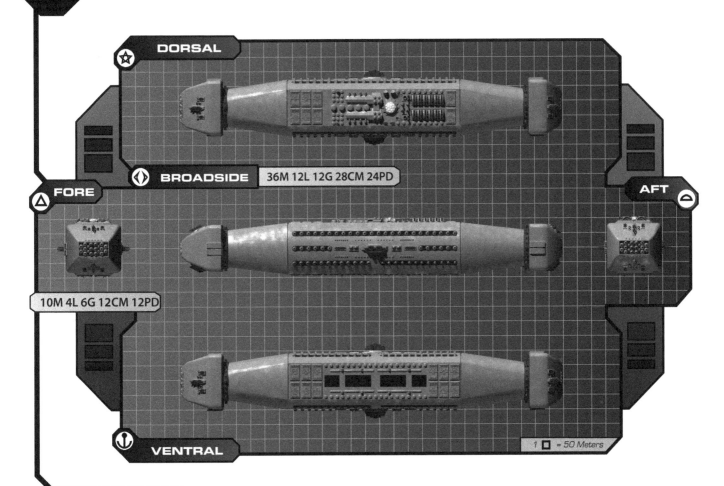

DORSAL

BROADSIDE
36M 12L 12G 28CM 24PD

FORE

AFT

10M 4L 6G 12CM 12PD

VENTRAL

1 ▢ = 50 Meters

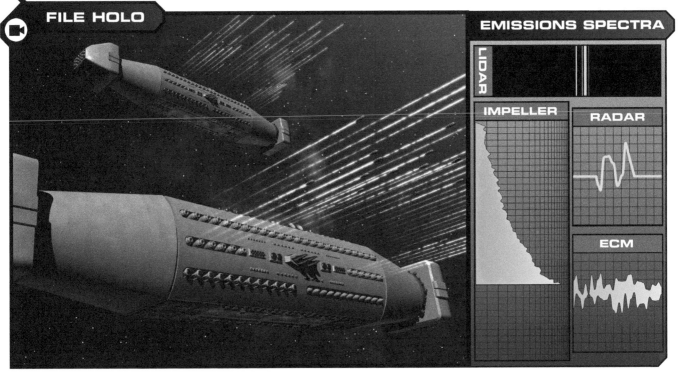

FILE HOLO

EMISSIONS SPECTRA

LIDAR

IMPELLER

RADAR

ECM

NOUVEAU PARIS-CLASS DREADNOUGHT

Ships in Class
Danville, Havensport, Juneau, Kaplin, Macrea's Tor, La Martin, Lafayette, Lutetia, Merston, Nouveau Paris, New Boston, Toulon, Tregizva, Waldensville

Estimated Service Life
1869 to 1987 PD

Specification
Mass: 6,331,500 tons
Length: 1,251 m
Beam: 181 m
Draught: 169 m
Acceleration: 426.7 G
Crew: 4257 (546 Officers, 3097 Enlisted, 614 Marines)
Power:
  5 RF/9 Golfech 5 Fusion Reactors
Electronics
  AG-6 Gravitic Detection Array
  AR-6 Phased Radar Array
  AL-4(c) Lidar Array
  SLCF-18(a) 116x104-channel Distributed Control System
  ARBB-19(b) Electronic Countermeasures
Armament:
  80 LM-8(b) Capital Ship Missile Tubes
  8 L/325 Capital Ship Lasers
  8 G/410 Grasers
  20 L/300 Capital Ship Lasers
  20 G/375 Grasers
  68 LMC-8(f) Counter Missile Tubes
  60 P/18x9 Laser Clusters
Magazines
  10032 L13(a) Capital Ship Missiles
  20468 C2 Counter Missiles
  20 LAD-5 Tethered ECM Decoys
Small Craft:
  4 DB.100 *Mercure*-class Cutters
  4 D.435 *Ouragan*-class Pinnaces
  2 DR.41 *Razzia*-class Assault Shuttles

Design and Construction
The *Nouveau Paris*-class dreadnought was originally designated as a "light superdreadnought" as a successor to the *Chevalier*-class. Designed in 1864 with an impressive 32 tube broadside, the *Nouveau Paris* had throw weight in excess of any of her contemporaries in her tonnage range, at the expense of hull armor. While the RMN tracks dreadnoughts as a distinct class from superdreadnoughts, the People's Navy sees the two classes as being mission oriented (where the mission is being a heavy wall of battle combatant), with tonnage ranges set by economics and likely deployment patterns, which blurs the distinction between the two in Havenite usage.

The *Nouveau Paris*-class has less magazine and bunkerage than a true superdreadnought, with the expectation being that it would be employed in a massive first strike doctrine against inferior foes. The lighter tonnage of this class was accepted for budgetary reasons, and expediency of construction and deployment—at the time of the *Nouveau Paris* commissioning, the ability to put a

squadron of capital ships into a system in short order was a higher priority than brute firepower, and when faced with foes built around battlecruisers or battleships, the *Nouveau Paris* is more than sufficient.

Production of the *Nouveau Paris*-class ceased as of the mid 1890s, a result of the People's Navy focusing on larger capital ships in anticipation of engaging the Star Kingdom of Manticore. The current estimates of capital ship counts as of the opening of hostilities is that the People's Navy has roughly 50 dreadnoughts, two squadrons of the *Chevalier*-class and four squadrons of the *Nouveau Paris*-class. As superdreadnought inventories increase, it's expected that the lighter capital ship units (other than the battleships used for interior defense and garrison duty) will eventually be decommissioned for budgetary reasons.

Over the service life of the *Nouveau Paris*-class dreadnoughts, the electronics have been refitted several times, and in the early 1880s, the defensive armament was adjusted to reflect the new reality of laser-head missiles.

Doctrinal Notes
The *Nouveau Paris*-class dreadnoughts are designed around winning the battle decisively in the first salvo; as the People's Navy moves into towed missile pods (after seeing them work for the Manticorans), it is expected that the *Nouveau Paris* will be upgraded with fire control sufficient to use them. The class, in spite of being a little light for superdreadnought duties, has its advocates in the design boards; many of them are attempting to get a superdreadnought class with 44 to 50 tube broadsides funded, with little avail.

Notable Units and Engagements
PNS *Tregizva*, under the command of Raoul LaFountaine, became the centerpiece of a critically acclaimed 16 hour holodrama that was a ratings smash, and caused a significant rise in volunteers for the People's Navy. Dramatizing the events of 1873, where *Tregizva* coordinated conquests of three different star systems, while also serving as an orbital medical facility providing support after a tsunami on a fourth, the ship maintained a reputation for always being in the right place at the right time, which Admiral LaFountaine credited with the operational planning departments giving him his orders. While *Tregizva* engaged in several battles in this time frame, most of them were lopsided affairs, until the last one, when a battlecruiser from the opposing side closed to suicidal ranges, and managed a freakish one-in-a-billion shot with a contact nuke down the throat, scraping off most of the superstructure on the top of the ship.

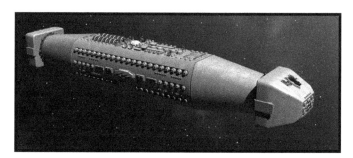

NOUVEAU PARIS - TECHNICAL READOUT

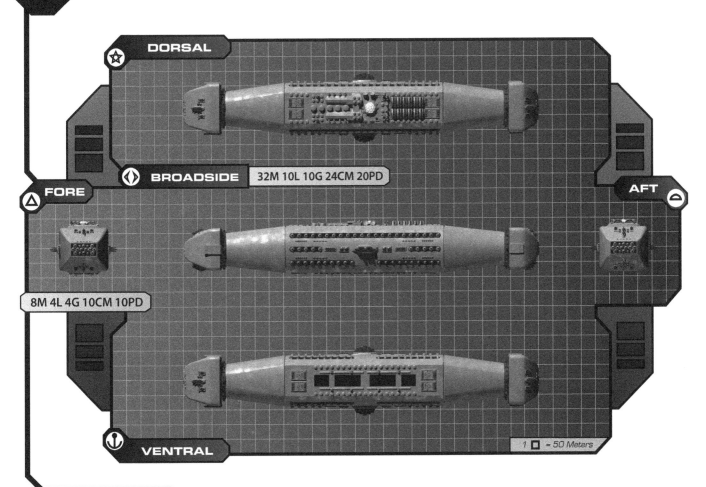

DORSAL

BROADSIDE 32M 10L 10G 24CM 20PD

FORE

AFT

8M 4L 4G 10CM 10PD

VENTRAL

1 □ = 50 Meters

FILE HOLO

EMISSIONS SPECTRA

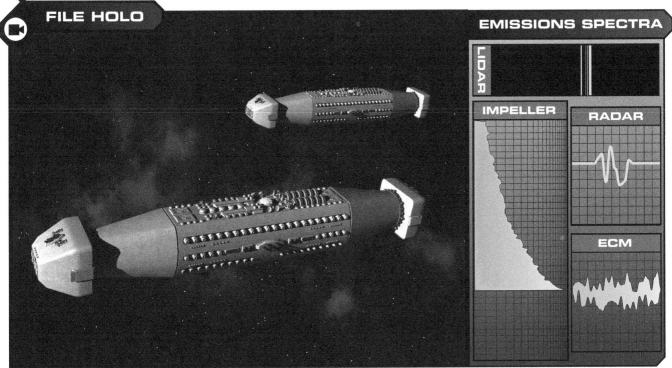

LIDAR

IMPELLER

RADAR

ECM

TRIUMPHANT-CLASS BATTLESHIP

Ships in Class
Admiral Quinterra, Conquerant, Conquistador, Schaumberg, Theban Warrior, Vindicator

Estimated Service Dates
1823 to 1956 PD

Specification
Mass: 4,493,250 tons
Length: 1,168 m
Beam: 159 m
Draught: 145 m
Acceleration: 445.1 G
Crew: 3876 (508 Officers, 2879 Enlisted, 489 Marines)
Power:
  4 RF/9 Golfech 2 Fusion Reactors
Electronics
  AG-1(c) Gravitic Detection Array
  AR-1 Phased Radar Array
  AL-2 Lidar Array
  SLCF-11 116-channel Fire Control System
  SDCC-11 104-channel Defensive Coordination and Control System
  ARBB-11(a) Electronic Countermeasures
Armament:
  76 LM-7(d) Capital Ship Missile Tubes
  4 L/300 Capital Ship Lasers
  4 G/398 Grasers
  12 L/280 Capital Ship Lasers
  12 G/357 Grasers
  44 LMC-8 Counter Missile Tubes
  52 P/16x8 Anti-Missile Lasers
Magazines:
  9096 L13(a) Capital Ship Missile
  13244 C2 Counter Missiles
  20 LAD-5 Tethered ECM Decoys
Small Craft:
  4 DB.100 *Mercure*-class Cutters
  8 D.450 *Ouragan*-class Pinnaces

Design and Construction
The most common class of capital ship in the People's Navy is the *Triumphant*-class battleship. Originally designed as a replacement for the aging *Fouchart*-class, the *Triumphants* evolved during their design phase from an update and revision of the class to something with much greater offensive punch. Since its introduction, the *Triumphant* has gone through four major revision cycles, and current construction is the Flight IV model, with substantially upgraded defensive fire control systems. There are currently two shipyards producing *Triumphants* in the People's Republic, while four others have since switched over to the newer *DuQuesne*-class superdreadnoughts.

While not considered a front-line unit, the *Triumphants* serve honorably as rear area defensive and pacification units, where their massive broadside makes them more than a match for any raiding battlecruisers. With no shortage of manpower, the People's Navy prefers to keep these units in commission as an insurance policy.

The *Triumphant's* offensive broadside is comparable to that of the *Nouveau Paris*-class dreadnought, though its defenses don't come close to a ship of that rate. Designed to have an overwhelming firepower advantage over any likely raiding force, offense was favored over defense; since battleships engaged by dreadnoughts and superdreadnoughts have low survivability rates, the expressed aim was to have a large enough broadside of missiles that it could at least wound a dreadnought before being taken down.

The downside of the *Triumphant's* broadside is its anemic energy weapon suite, and its sub-par active defenses; a *Triumphant* CO wants to avoid the extended missile range duel against another capital ship, trying to close vectors for a medium range engagement while avoiding the close-in raking fire of beams, which is a tricky piece of handling to perform on a ship with a paltry 445 G acceleration.

Doctrinal Notes
Battleships in the People's Navy, in spite of their role as second line and rear area defensive units, get an aggressive refit schedule. In particular, new countermissile and point defense cluster upgrades get put on the *Triumphants* before other capital units, because the *Triumphants* are generally deployed closer to the shipyards, and because they rely far more heavily on their active defenses than they do on their armor or sidewalls for survivability. This also gives an extensive class of ships for working up trials on new systems for capital ships.

Notable Units and Battles
PNS *Conquistador* is the with the longest continuous record of "Double A" efficiency ratings in the People's Navy, having achieved that heady mark for 19 consecutive years, and four different commanding officers. With a patrol zone covering seven star systems on the Solarian League edge of Havenite space, *Conquistador* has seen only limited engagements, mostly against battlecruisers and smaller. In 1897 PD, *Conquistador* encountered a secessionist conspiracy. Her captain, Henry Thurber, detached his destroyers as screening units and took *Conquistador* to the edge of the hyper limit. With very careful use of timing and tight beam coordination with his screen, he was able to make multiple hyperspace transitions at different points around the Morell system, falling on two battlecruisers by comparative surprise. With the destruction of the two battlecruisers, Thurber was able to decisively end the space-based portion of the conflict.

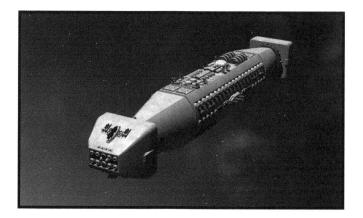

TRIUMPHANT - TECHNICAL READOUT

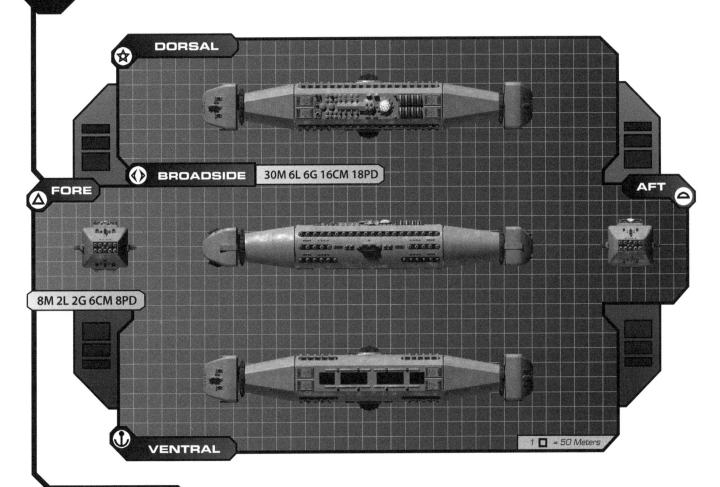

DORSAL

BROADSIDE 30M 6L 6G 16CM 18PD

FORE

AFT

8M 2L 2G 6CM 8PD

VENTRAL

1 ☐ = 50 Meters

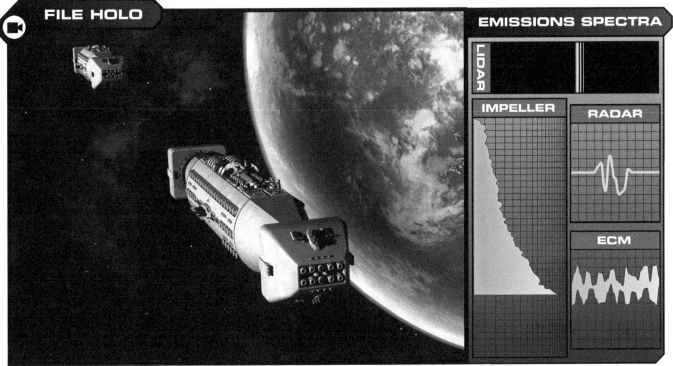

FILE HOLO

EMISSIONS SPECTRA

LIDAR

IMPELLER

RADAR

ECM

SULTAN-CLASS BATTLECRUISER

Ships in Class
Abdali, Achmed, Alp Arslan, Bayezid, Fatih, Isa, Kerebin, Malik, Mehmed, Murad, Musa, Rash al-Din, Saladin, Selim, Sinjar, Sulieman, Sultan, Tinaly, Tolek, Walid, Yavuz, Yildirim

Estimated Service Dates
1892 - 1926 P.D.

Specification
Mass: 859,250 tons
Length: 707 m
Beam: 90 m
Draught: 80 m
Acceleration: 489.2 G
Total Crew: 2195 (190 Officers, 1705 Enlisted, 300 Marines)
Power:
  3 RF/8 Tricastin 2 Fusion Reactors
Electronics:
  AG-15 Gravitic Detection Array
  AR-18(a) Phased Radar Array
  AL-13 Lidar Array
  SLCF-19(a) 54x40channel Distributed Control System
  ARBB-23 Electronic Countermeasures
Armament:
  46 LMF-5(d) Missile Tubes
  4 L/130 Capital Ship Lasers
  12 L/118 Anti-Ship Lasers
  12 G/125 Grasers
  40 LMC-8(g) Counter Missile Tubes
  36 P/18x6 Anti-Missile Lasers
Magazines:
  1528 F17 Impeller Drive Missile
  3640 C2 Counter Missiles
  10 LAD-15 Tethered ECM Decoys
Small Craft:
  4 D.435 *Ouragan*-class Pinnaces
  5 DB.100 *Mercure*-class Cutters

Design and Construction
The *Sultan*-class battlecruiser is the newest in the People's Navy. It is almost ten percent larger then its predecessor, the *Tiger*-class, and boasts significant enhancements in both armament and electronics over the older design.

As with other battlecruisers in the People's Navy, the *Sultan* is designed to operate in conjunction with a fleet, tightly coordinated into the wall of battle. Havenite doctrine treats battlecruisers as very small capital ships, rather than "large cruisers". The wisdom of such a doctrine is considered suspect, due to lighter missile broadsides and less powerful energy weapons.

The *Sultan* has a designated endurance of only 95 days between refueling stops, nearly twenty-five percent less than that of the *Reliant* class used by the RMN, with the mass freed up from reduced bunkerage used for larger magazines. In its doctrinal role, working as part of a main battle force, rather than in commerce interdiction squadrons, this trade-off makes sense.

While all navies attempt to build ships around modular components in the interest of reducing maintenance and making class-wide refits simpler, the practice falls short of the theory once real engineering takes over from plans drawn in a holotank. Interestingly enough, the *Sultan*-class comes closer than most. While this requires a somewhat larger store of spares to provide redundancy in critical systems, it has made for excellent cost savings and reduced yard time during maintenance and refits. The rapid pace of the initial phases of the war have caused some concern, as the *Sultans* have run ahead of their spare parts train, causing some logistics issues. Shortages in component supply and the incredible difficulty of station repairs when the necessary modules are unavailable have left many units with serious flaws in their readiness reports.

Doctrinal Notes
Sultans rarely operate as singletons. Designed to stand in the wall of battle, they are most often used as squadron flagships. When operating on detached duty, they are usually assigned in division strength at a minimum.

On the rare cases where the People's Navy embarks on raiding missions, they prefer to operate in squadron strength or above, ensuring an overwhelming superiority against the defending forces.

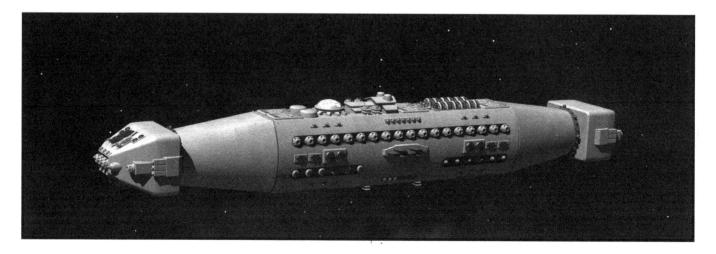

SULTAN - TECHNICAL READOUT

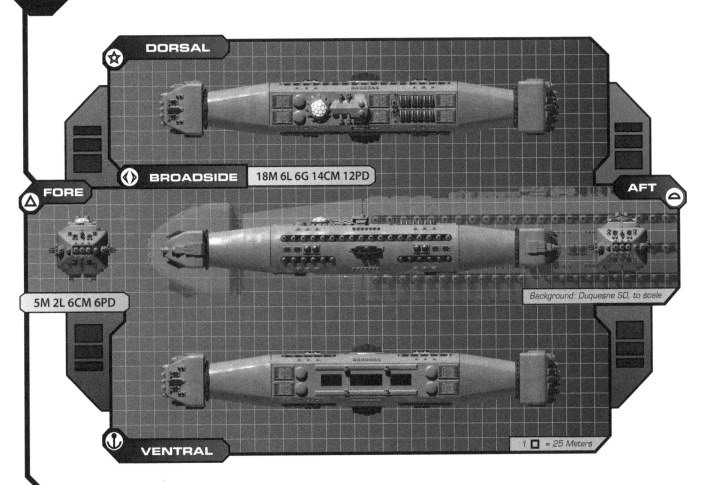

✪ DORSAL

◈ BROADSIDE 18M 6L 6G 14CM 12PD

△ FORE

⬠ AFT

Background: Duquesne SD, to scale

5M 2L 6CM 6PD

⚓ VENTRAL

1 ⬜ = 25 Meters

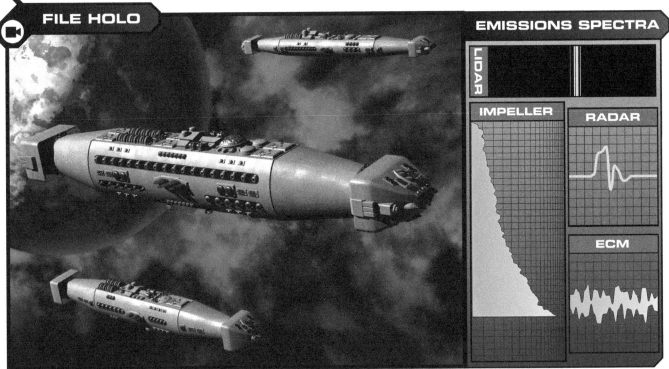

📹 FILE HOLO

EMISSIONS SPECTRA

LIDAR

IMPELLER

RADAR

ECM

TIGER-CLASS BATTLECRUISER

Ships in Class
Bengal, Bobcat, Burmese, Cheetah, Cougar, Jaguar, Leopard, Lion, Lioness, Lynx, Manx, Mountain Lion, Ocelot, Panther, Puma, Sabretooth, Tiger, Wildcat

Estimated Service Life
1861 PD to 1925 PD

Specification
Mass: 734,500 tons
Length: 671 m
Beam: 85 m
Draught: 76 m
Acceleration: 493.0 G
Crew: 1927 (244 Officers, 1383 Enlisted, 300 Marines)
Power:
  3 RF/8 Areva 2 Fusion Reactors
Electronics
  AG-11(d) Gravitic Detection Array
  AR-15 Phased Radar Array
  AL-16(b) Lidar Array
  SLCF-18 46x40-channel Distributed Control System
  ARBB-19 Electronic Countermeasures
Armament:
  40 LMF-5(b) Missile Tubes
  2 G/140 Grasers
  10 L/118 Anti-Ship Lasers
  10 G/125 Grasers
  32 LMC-8(f) Counter Missile Tubes
  28 P/18x6 Anti-Missile Lasers
Magazines
  1168 F17 Impeller Drive Missiles
  3616 C2 Counter Missiles
  8 LAD-15 Tethered ECM Decoys
Small Craft:
  2 DB.100 Mercure-class Cutters
  4 D.435 Ouragan-class Pinnaces

Design and Construction Notes
The Tiger-class battlecruiser is the largest class of battlecruisers in the People's Navy. The class is expected to last well into the mid 1920's.

The Tiger-class was designed in 1861 to replace the aging Tonnerre-class as the next generation of escorts for battle squadrons. Designed to integrate tightly into the wall of battle, the bunkerage on Tigers was reduced to match the ships it'd be assigned with, and per Havenite doctrine, was assumed to have a logistics train attached to the task force, with the space freed up used to enhance the total armament package of the class. Deployments were short and never far from supply or a major fleet base. Havenite doctrine focuses on winning wars in a short period of time with overwhelming force, making the cramped conditions on the Tiger-class bearable for its standard deployments.

While the newer Sultan-class has limited ability for independent operations, Tigers seldom operate alone due to crowding and short endurance. As the conflict with the Star Kingdom of Manticore has heated up, Tiger deployments have grown longer, and forward deployments have become distressingly common, limiting access to off-ship entertainment for the crew. Readiness levels have suffered as a result, and the navy has been cycling Tigers to the rear areas with each new Sultan commissioned.

While older and less capable than the Sultan-class in terms of throw weight, the Tiger-class is a dangerous opponent. The fire control system has been completely replaced in the last refit series and an enhanced ECM package is being phased in over the next two years. Sidewall strength is an issue, with little or no room for the new equipment necessary. However, the Tiger-class is almost as heavily armored as the Sultan, with bulkheads and compartmentalization rarely seen on a ship of its size.

Like the Sultans, the Tiger-class has deep magazines on the broadsides with shallower magazines for the chase armament. This supports their role as battle squadron escorts, and further hampers their ability to operate independently. One design proposal put forward as part of the recent Service Life Extension Program is to reduce the magazine levels in the broadside in favor of an additional set of sidewall generators, and additional bunkerage. The first ships refitted to this standard are due to hit the slipways in 1905. Their combat performance will determine if the changes are propagated to the rest of the class.

Doctrinal Notes
While the Sultan-class has been in service just over a decade, there are still numerous Tigers in forward deployments, usually in mixed squadrons with Sultan, or as direct attachments to larger formations built around superdreadnoughts. In rear deployments, they're found operating in homogeneous squadrons or, less often, with the older Tonnerre-class.

A number of Tigers have participated in recent raids on Alliance territory, though the bulk of the Tigers have been forward deployed to supply and logistics bases to act as reaction forces in case of raids by the Alliance.

Notable Units and Engagements
PNS Leopard was delivered over six months late, due to serious problems in the heat management system that required near bulkhead-to-bulkhead replacement of the top deck of the ship. After this delay in working up, the ship was short stopped from its deployment with the 16th Battlecruiser Squadron to fill a slot in an important convoy to the Silesian Confederacy. A few days into the three month journey, an explosion in one of the waste processing units shut down half of the ships' life support and water recycling.

The damage was quickly repaired, but due to some fault in the processing system and the cramped design, the waste processing system began to vent into the atmosphere recycling system. For the remainder of the deployment, despite numerous repairs, the entire ship smelled of sewage, overlaid by floral aerosols.

While the problem was finally tracked down and fixed at the end of the deployment, Leopard has never lived down the reputation. To this day PNS "Litterbox" is still beset with annoying, though generally non life threatening maintenance issues.

TIGER - TECHNICAL READOUT

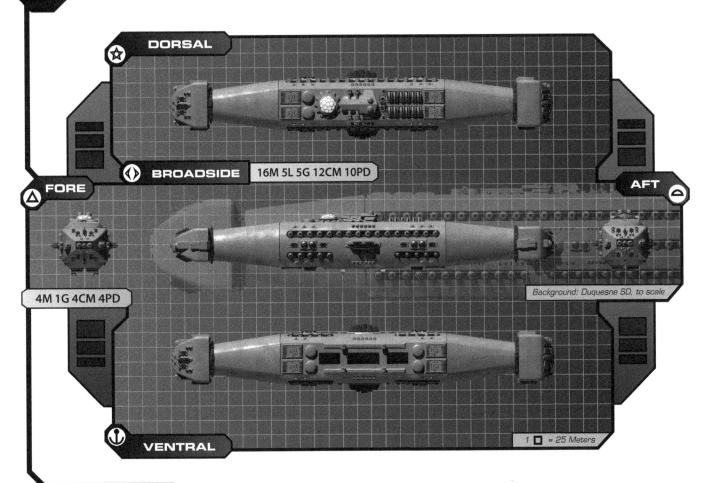

DORSAL

BROADSIDE 16M 5L 5G 12CM 10PD

FORE

AFT

4M 1G 4CM 4PD

Background: Duquesne SD, to scale

VENTRAL

1 ☐ = 25 Meters

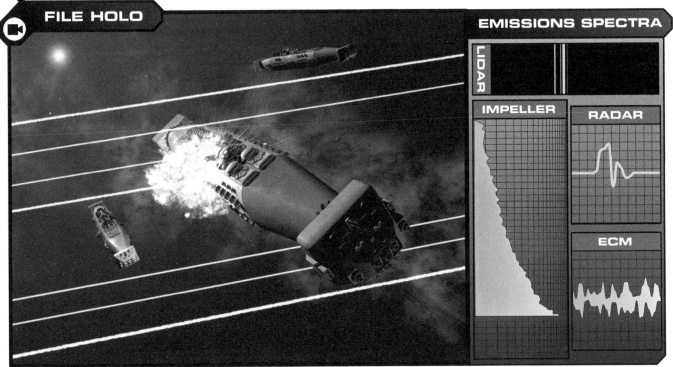

FILE HOLO

EMISSIONS SPECTRA

LIDAR

IMPELLER

RADAR

ECM

MARS-B CLASS HEAVY CRUISER

Ships in Class
Anhur, Ares, De Conde, Hachiman, Huan-Ti, Ishtar, Rienzi, Tanit

Estimated Service Dates
1905 to 1957 PD

Specification
Mass: 477,250 tons
Length: 607 m
Beam: 73 m
Draught: 61 m
Acceleration: 501.1 G
Crew: 1193 (100 Officers, 897 Enlisted, 196 Marines,)
Power:
　2 Goshawk-3 Fusion Reactors
Electronics:
　AG-16(a) Gravitic Detection Array
　AR-19 Phased Radar Array
　AL-14 Lidar Array
　SLCF-20 70x40-channel Distributed Control System
　ARBB-25 Electronic Countermeasures
Armament:
　28 LMF-5(d) Missile Tubes
　6 G/125 Grasers
　24 L/101 Anti-Ship Lasers
　32 LMC-8(g) Counter Missile Tubes
　32 P/16x5 Laser Clusters
Magazines:
　336 F17 Impeller Drive Missile
　1568 C2 Counter Missiles
　12 LAD-17(a) Tethered ECM Decoys
Small Craft:
　3 D.435 Ouragan-class Pinnaces
　5 DB.100 Mercure-class Cutters

Design and Construction
The Mars-B design quickly superseded the original Mars-class heavy cruiser (later referred to as the Mars-A-class) which was developed as a replacement for the disappointing Sword-class. The Mars-B program reduced the internal magazines from twenty-two rounds per launcher to only twelve. While this limits the endurance in a sustained engagement, the mass saved allowed the Mars-B to literally double the energy broadside from the original design and significantly upgrade its defenses.

Unlike the Mars-A, the Mars-B class mounts the new Goshawk-three fusion reactors. The Goshawk-three is substantially more efficient than its predecessors, producing almost twice the output for a bare ten percent increase in size. This increased output allows the Mars-B to operate on a single reactor in an emergency. The mass saved by eliminating the third reactor was used to mount an even heavier armament.

The most significant upgrade on the Mars-B is the ability to control towed missile pods. The ability to fire a massive opening salvo is the logical extension of the Republic's "massive first strike" doctrine, shown by the Conquerer-class.

Unlike its predecessor, the Mars-B is one of the first classes to incorporate updated electronic systems courtesy of the first technology transfers from the Solarian League. Overall, the Mars-B class clearly indicates the People's Navy's desire to design increased survivability into their heavy cruisers.

Doctrinal Notes
The designers felt the reduction in magazine space over the original design was justified, as the Mars-B is the first class with sufficient fire control to fire their newly developed missile pods. Commanders who have to husband their shots, or find themselves madly charging through a missile broadside with empty magazines disagree, but do so quietly, lest they seem disloyal.

The Office of Planning anticipates using pods and first-strike tactics to break up Manticoran squadron and task force anti-missile defensive organization. With the massive strikes they intend to fire from towed pods, they feel that they can sacrifice more of the new class's internal missile power in favor of the combination of improved defenses and a more powerful energy armament.

Production delays in the missile pods have slowed their release into widespread use, and as of this writing, neither the class itself, nor the newly developed doctrine has been tested in battle.

Notable Units and Battles
None of the first flight Mars-B units have seen combat as of this writing, due to the tragic loss of PNS Tanit while in parking orbit around Enki. From all accounts, Tanit was under standby power levels when she had a glitch in the containment bottle of her number two reactor. Tanit herself was completely destroyed. The remaining units built at the same yard been pulled from active service while the incident is being investigated. They are expected to return to duty in 1906 to 1907.

MARS-B - TECHNICAL READOUT

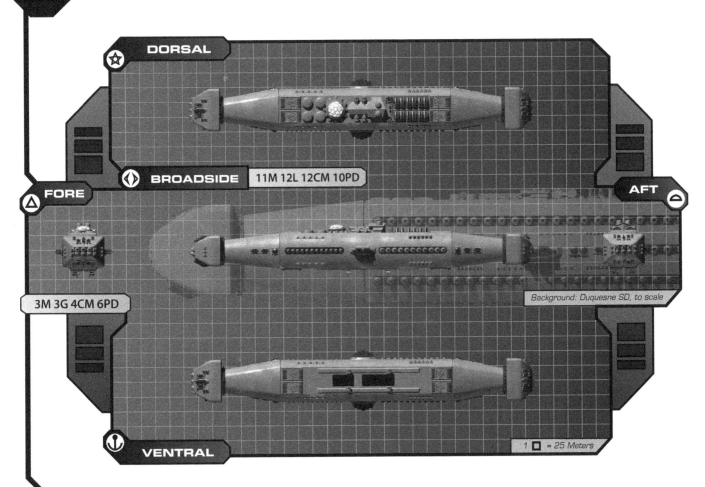

DORSAL

BROADSIDE   11M 12L 12CM 10PD

FORE   AFT

3M 3G 4CM 6PD

Background: Duquesne SD, to scale

VENTRAL

1 ☐ = 25 Meters

FILE HOLO

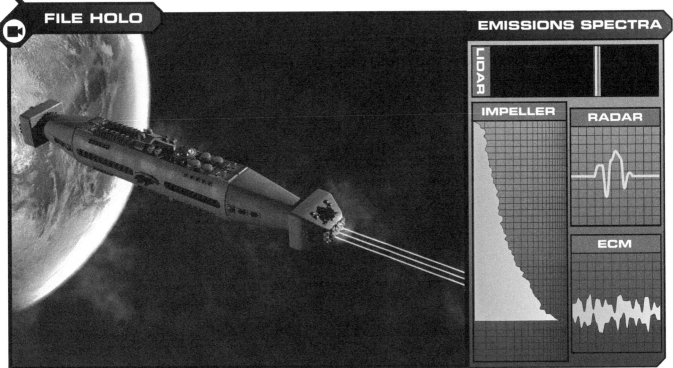

EMISSIONS SPECTRA

LIDAR

IMPELLER   RADAR

ECM

MARS-A CLASS HEAVY CRUISER

Ships in Class
Loki, Mars, Marduk, Nurghal, Odin, Thor, Tyr

Estimated Service Life
1896 to 1952 PD

Specification
Mass: 451,750 tons
Length: 607 m
Beam: 73 m
Draught: 61 m
Acceleration: 501.1 G
Crew: 1086 (119 Officers, 671 Enlisted, 296 Marines)
Power:
  2 Goshawk 2 Fusion Reactors
Electronics
  AG-16 Gravitic Detection Array
  AR-19 Phased Radar Array
  AL-14 Lidar Array
  SLCF-19(b) 70x40-channel Distributed Control System
  ARBB-23(b) Electronic Countermeasures
Armament:
  28 LMF-5(d) Missile Tubes
  6 G/125 Grasers
  12 L/101 Anti-Ship Lasers
  32 LMC-8(g) Counter Missile Tubes
  32 P/16x5 Laser Clusters
Magazines
  616 F17 Impeller Drive Missile
  1664 C2 Counter Missiles
  12 LAD-17 Tethered ECM Decoys
Small Craft:
  3 D.435 *Ouregan*-class Pinnaces
  5 DB.100 *Mercure*-class Cutters

Design and Construction
The original *Mars*-class of heavy cruiser was a replacement for the 286,000 ton (and disappointing) *Sword*-class. A revolutionary design, the *Mars* blurs somewhat the boundary between heavy cruiser and battlecruiser; at almost 50% greater tonnage than other heavy cruisers, the *Mars* was a beast of a ship, boasting 11 tube missile broadsides, extensive defenses, and deep magazines and bunkerage to enable long cruises. The *Mars* series was the first PN design to use the Goshawk series of fusion reactors. The *Mars* is able to run on one reactor in an emergency, and only carries two, rather than the PN's usual reactor count of three.

It was also something of a slipway queen, with constant problems related to the impeller nodes and compensator, which were both uprated from the ones on the *Sword*-class. The initial impeller specification was capable of pushing a 450,000 ton ship at cruiser accelerations; it just couldn't do it with the PN's usual requirements for uptime and service life, and required scandalous amounts of maintenance hours to keep running.

This, and the re-introduction of towed missile pods, were the two primary factors leading to the *Mars-B*. With the advent of the *Mars-B*, the *Mars* was re-designated the *Mars-A*. The biggest difference between the *Mars-A* and *Mars-B* is in the broadside beam armament (the *B* has almost twice the beam firepower). The *Mars-A*, with an identical hull, has over twice the magazine capacity and is built for a sustained conventional engagement, while the *Mars-B* sacrificed magazine space for greater beam armament and durability, on the theory that its missile armament could be optimized for towed pods and a heavy initial salvo.

Doctrinal Notes
In most ways, the *Mars-A* serves as a giant heavy cruiser, with heavy throw weights and deep magazines for a sustained fight. They are part of the natural progression of the Havenite "win the first salvo" doctrine. The *Mars-B* carries this doctrine to its logical conclusion with towed missile pods, an innovation that should be entering service within the next T-year.

The *Mars-As* have been relegated to lower intensity combat roles because of their inability to handle towed pods, and are expected to be retained in the inventory as a "second rate" cruiser for the next 50 years or so.

MARS-A – TECHNICAL READOUT

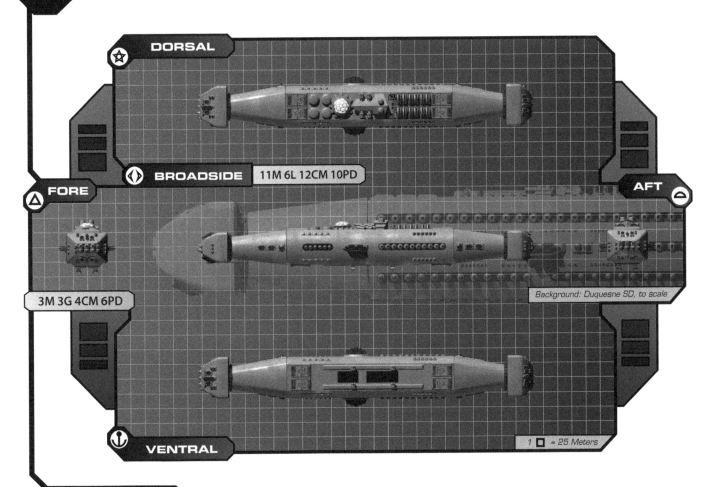

DORSAL

BROADSIDE 11M 6L 12CM 10PD

FORE

AFT

3M 3G 4CM 6PD

Background: Duquesne SD, to scale

VENTRAL

1 ☐ = 25 Meters

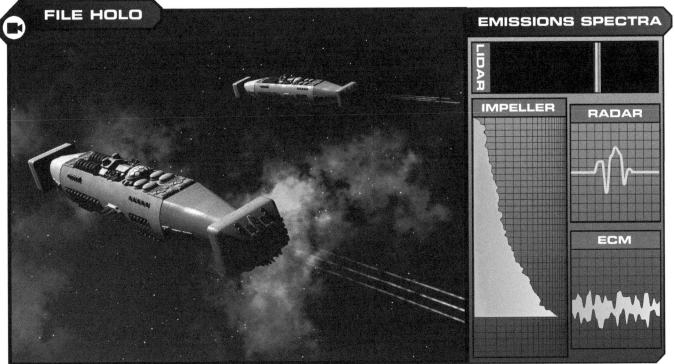

FILE HOLO

EMISSIONS SPECTRA

LIDAR

IMPELLER

RADAR

ECM

SWORD-CLASS HEAVY CRUISER

Ships in Class
Claymore, Cutlass, Dirk, Drusus, Durandal, Epee, Estoc, Excalibur, Falchion, Flamberge, Foil, Gladius, Jian, Katana, Khopesh, Poignard, Raiden, Rapier, Sabre, Scimitar, Shamshir, Sword, Wakasashi

Expected Service Life
1867 to 1919 PD

Specification
Mass: 286,250 tons
Length: 512 m
Beam: 62 m
Draught: 52 m
Acceleration: 510.2 G
Total Crew: 960 (77 Officers, 693 Enlisted, 190 Marines)
Power:
  2 RF/7 Chinon 3 Fusion Reactors
Electronics
  AG-12 Gravitic Detection Array
  AR-15 Phased Radar Array
  AL-16(c) Lidar Array
  SLCF-18 24x18-channel Distributed Control System
  ARBB-19(a) Electronic Countermeasures
Armament:
  18 LMF-5(c) High-Speed Missile Tubes
  2 L/130 Capital Ship Lasers
  10 L/118 Anti-Ship Lasers
  18 LMC-8(f) Counter Missile Tubes
  22 P/16x5 Laser Clusters
Magazines:
  324 F17 Impeller Drive Missile
  360 C2 Counter Missiles
  8 LAD-17 Tethered ECM Decoys
Small Craft:
  2 D.435 *Ouragan* class Pinnaces
  3 DB.100 *Mercure* class Cutters

Design and Construction
The *Sword*-class heavy cruiser is an older design, first proposed in 1864 as a replacement for the *Champion*-class, the last unit of which was decommissioned in 1871.

The design of the *Sword* is an even more extreme case of the heavy missile-design philosophy used in the *Bastogne*-class destroyer.

The *Sword*-class does correct some of the shortcomings of the *Bastogne* by accepting a lighter broadside throw weight in favor of larger magazines. However, its countermissile magazines hold less than a third of the ammunition they need to last through a typical engagement.

The *Sword*-class is the only ship in the People's Navy to mount the LMF-5(c) missile tube. The LMF-5(c) has a faster cycle time than most launchers, at a cost in reliability and service life. The problem lies in the high-speed loading mechanism, which has a tendency to freeze unexpectedly when shuffling a full magazine queue. Many captains have learned to fill their magazines one to three rounds short of the nominal rated load to help mitigate this problem.

There have been several modifications and refits to the class, all of which attempted to address the countermissile shortcomings by providing additional counter-missiles magazine space, usually at the expense of removing energy weapons or reducing offensive missile tubes. None of them has been satisfactory, however, wartime experience indicated that you simply could not build an effective heavy cruiser on under 300,000 tons with current-generation Havenite hardware.

Doctrinal Notes
While the *Sword*-class has the magazine space for several minutes of sustained fire, its critical shortage of countermissiles force it to seek a decisive advantage early in the battle. It is not designed as a close combatant, but most captains will try to close the range quickly to give then the best targeting solution to compensate for the older fire control systems.

By the time the range has closed, the *Sword* must rely on the quick cycle time of its launchers to overwhelm the target with rapid continuous fire. Given that the *Sword* will most likely have depleted its countermissile magazines by that time, its only hope is to destroy the opponent before it is destroyed itself.

Notable Units and Battles
The most successful of the refit proposal was the one that used PNS *Flamberge* as a test bed. Rather than reduce the energy armament, with the associated decrease in defensive effectiveness, the engineers segmented off portions of the offensive magazines and used the space for additional countermissile magazines. While it gave *Flamberge* almost twice the endurance on its countermissile launchers, routing the countermissile ammunition through the already unreliable ship-killer magazine systems resulted in frequent jams, that could disable both launcher types fed by the same missile handling queue.

SWORD - TECHNICAL READOUT

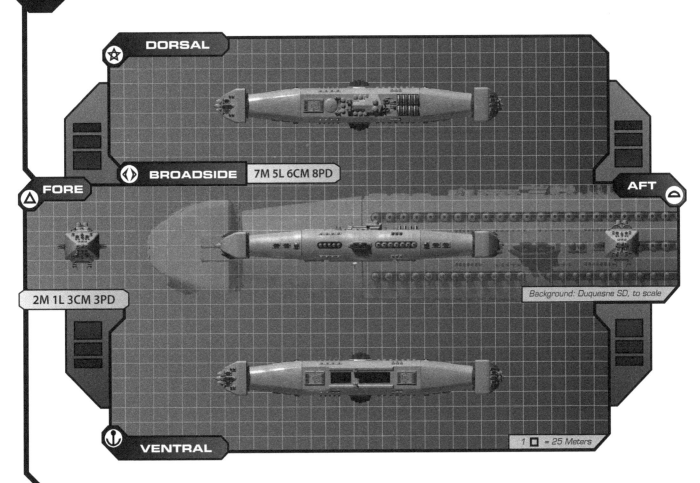

DORSAL

BROADSIDE 7M 5L 6CM 8PD

FORE

AFT

2M 1L 3CM 3PD

Background: Duquesne SD, to scale

VENTRAL

1 ☐ = 25 Meters

FILE HOLO

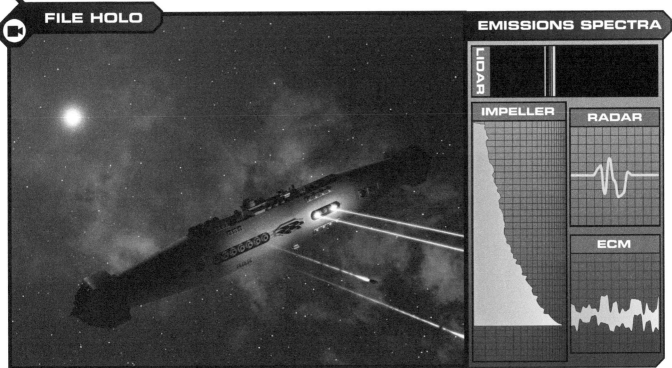

EMISSIONS SPECTRA

LIDAR

IMPELLER

RADAR

ECM

CHARLES WADE POPE-CLASS LIGHT CRUISER

Ships in Class

Marcus Beaudway, Thomas Fischer, William Harting, Isaiah Kenter, Joseph T. Marrone, Kenneth Nastansky, Charles Wade Pope, Esperanza deSouza

Estimated Service Life

1872 to 1923 PD

Specification

Mass: 125,250 tons
Length: 437 m
Beam: 45 m
Draught: 35 m
Acceleration: 517.8 G
Crew: 457 (69 Officers, 388 Enlisted)
Power:
  2 RF/6 Dampierre 4 Fusion Reactors
Electronics
  AG-24 Gravitic Detection Array
  AR-25(a) Phased Radar Array
  AL-25 Lidar Array
  SLCF-18(a) 22x12-channel Distributed Control System
  ARBB-20 Electronic Countermeasures
Armament:
  16 LME-3(b) Missile Tubes
  2 L/75 Anti-Ship Lasers
  10 L/66 Anti-Ship Lasers
  10 LMC-8(g) Counter Missile Tubes
  10 P/16x3 Laser Clusters
Magazines:
  280 E14 Impeller Drive Missiles
  410 C2 Counter Missiles
  6 LAD-24 Tethered ECM Decoys
Small Craft:
  3 DB.100 *Mercure*-class Cutters
  2 D.435 *Ouragan*-class Pinnaces

Design and Construction

The *Charles Wade Pope*-class Light Cruiser is the most extreme example of corrupt politicking in the creation of ships in the People's Navy. Like the *Desforge*-class, the *Pope* was built at the behest of Legislaturalists funneling building contracts to specific shipyards, most of which were owned in part by family interests related to the politicians involved.

Unlike the *Desforge*, the *Pope* was built as an attempt to duplicate the *Liberty*-class light cruisers of the Solarian League navy; three *Liberties* were purchased from the SLN's mothballed inventory. The line of reasoning behind the purchase was that, even stripped as an export model ship, enough of the Solarian League's technology and procedures would still be present for copying into future designs.

The designed ship was smaller than the *Conqueror*, with roughly the same defensive suite, and a modest reduction in broadside capabilities. Like SLN designs, the *Pope* carries an extensive array of decoys and recon drones, more so than is typical for a cruiser of its mass in the People's Navy. Budget cuts during development resulted in the reduction of the broadside and a slight reduction

in the magazine capacity of the ship, though it did not result in a reduction in the most controversial aspect of the design—the spacious and "overly comfortable" berthing for enlisted personnel, including twice the number of showers, and a far larger allotment of off-duty recreational spaces. This has caused commanders who have taken personnel drafts off of *Popes* to grumble about the amenities "softening the crews" to the point where they need to be toughened up.

Doctrinal Notes

The *Pope* is meant to be a true cruiser, with long cruise endurance. This puts it somewhat at odds with the PN's typical light cruiser deployment, as missile platforms in the screen around a heavier nucleus of battlecruisers. Because of the mismatch of capabilities and standard doctrine, and a scandal in the procurement process, only two squadrons of *Popes* were actually built. After an independent investigation committee resolves the procurement scandal, it is estimated that the *Popes* will be put back into limited production.

Notable Units and Engagements

One notable *Pope* was PNS *Jonathan Talbott*, which has the distinction of being the only ship in the People's Navy to have visited every single planet of the People's Republic of Haven, though this distinction took place over 14 years and 8 commanding officers.

Talbott's original deployment put it in the quadrant of Havenite space near the Solarian League. With most of that region well assimilated into the People's Republic, *Talbott* performed show the flag missions, and "visible piracy deterrence" for shipping going through that part of space; through happenstance and orders, *Talbott* had been routed through most of the systems in the Republic over the next decade, and then attached to the mop up forces pacifying new conquests. When official notice of the ship's distinction occurred, *Talbott* was conspicuously assigned to carry routine message traffic to new conquests as something of a "good luck charm", most recently to Clairmond, Treadway, Solway and Seaford 9. The crew of *Talbott* take pride in their "flag wall", which carries mementoes from each planet visited by the crew.

POPE - TECHNICAL READOUT

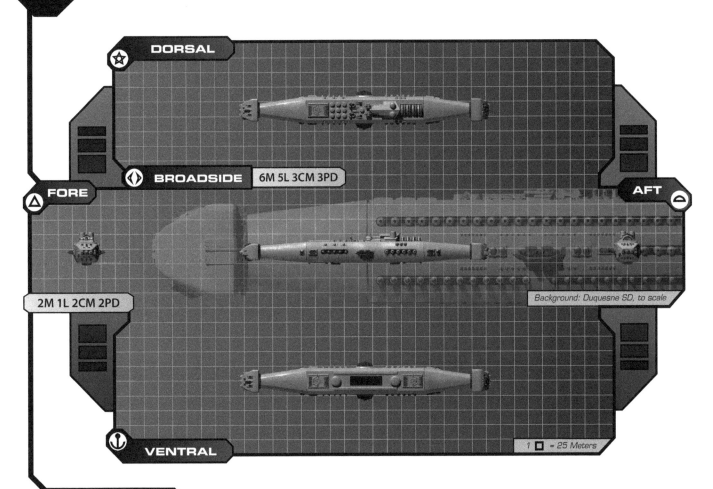

DORSAL

BROADSIDE | 6M 5L 3CM 3PD

FORE

AFT

Background: Duquesne SD, to scale

2M 1L 2CM 2PD

1 ☐ = 25 Meters

VENTRAL

FILE HOLO

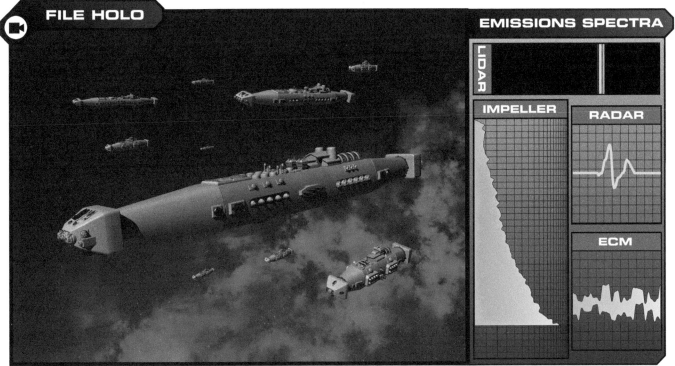

EMISSIONS SPECTRA

LIDAR

IMPELLER

RADAR

ECM

CONQUEROR-CLASS LIGHT CRUISER

Ships in Class

Alexander, Alvarado, Babar, Caesar, Cortés, Diaz, Khan, Hannibal, Hideyoshi, Huangdi, Montezuma, Napoleon, Rameses, Valdivia, Vaubon, Wari, William

Service Life

1895 to 1967 PD

Specification

Mass: 145,000 tons
Length: 459 m
Beam: 48 m
Draught: 37 m
Acceleration: 516.9 G
Crew: 476 (48 Officers, 428 Enlisted)
Power:
  2 RF/6 Phenix 1 Fusion Reactors
Electronics:
  AG-26 Gravitic Detection Array
  AR-26(b) Phased Radar Array
  AL-27 Lidar Array
  SLCF-19(b) 22x12-channel Distributed Control System
  ARBB-23 Electronic Countermeasures
Armament:
  22 LME-3(d) Missile Tubes
  2 L/75 Anti-Ship Lasers
  12 L/62 Anti-Ship Lasers
  12 LMC-8(g) Counter Missile Tubes
  10 P/16x3 Laser Clusters
Magazines:
  352 E14 Impeller Drive Missiles
  372 C2 Counter Missiles
  8 LAD-24 Tethered ECM Decoys
Small Craft:
  2 D.450 *Ouragan*-class Pinnaces
  3 DB.100 *Mercure*-class Cutters

Design and Construction

The *Conqueror*-class light cruiser is the product of refinements to the same design program as the *Bastogne*-class destroyer. Taking lessons learned from the *Bastogne*, the office of shipbuilding requested proposals for a long-range combatant with stronger defensive and close range firepower.

While significantly larger as the *Bastogne*, the *Conqueror* mounts only one more missile tube per broadside than the smaller ship,

the rest of the mass is used for a respectable broadside energy suite and chase armaments, adequate defenses and a significant increase in magazine space. Overall, the *Conqueror* is a solid design suited for a variety of missions.

Doctrinal Notes

The *Conqueror*-class represents the current doctrine of the People's Navy. Known to some as "The Battle for the First Salvo," the fundamental tactic is to overwhelm the opponent with a heavy initial series of salvos fired with the minimum cycle time. It is a crude, brute force solution to the technical advantages of Manticoran hardware, but remains fundamentally sound, provided sufficient weight of fire can be massed against the enemy. The drawbacks of this strategy are that a *Conqueror* class ship can find itself short on magazine capacity, particularly on a deep strike mission where it must engage multiple targets before linking up with ammunition hauler. The *Conqueror's* extensive close in armament serves as a deterrent, as no light cruiser really likes the idea of being in beam range.

Current doctrine is to engage the enemy at three-to-one or better odds whenever possible, given the individual capabilities of the two navies. For this reason, *Conquerors* rarely operate in less than divisional strength, and are more often deployed as "short" squadrons of 6-8 units. Accompanied by *Bastognes* and *Swords*, the *Conqueror* makes up the core of the People's Navy's light units used in the current confrontations with Manticore.

Notable Units and Battles

The most well-known *Conqueror*-class unit in the People's Navy would have to be PNS *Hideyoshi*. Under the command of Captain Paul Burke, *Hideyoshi* was deployed in the Verde sector in 1886 P.D. on routine antipiracy patrols. During the next eight T-months, Captain Burke displayed uncanny luck in his ability to identify slavers. *Hideyoshi* captured no less than three Mesa-run slave ships during that time period, two of which were carrying full loads of human 'cargo' to be delivered. The final ship was caught just after delivery, allowing Burke to identify and bring into custody the local system governor responsible for the trade.

Hideyoshi was last seen in Alto Verde in 1887, as she departed on the back sweep of her patrol pattern. She never reached her destination, and is listed as lost to causes unknown.

Unsubstantiated reports of *Conquerors* being sold into second tier navies continue to crop up in intelligence reports.

CONQUEROR - TECHNICAL READOUT

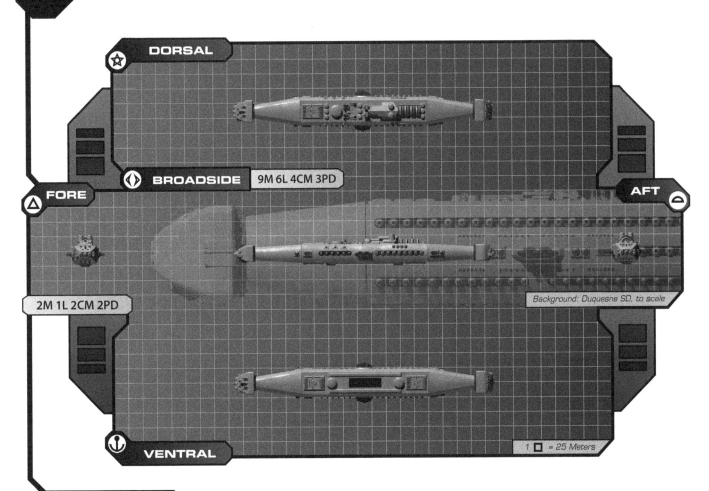

DORSAL

BROADSIDE 9M 6L 4CM 3PD

FORE

AFT

2M 1L 2CM 2PD

Background: Duquesne SD, to scale

VENTRAL

1 ▢ = 25 Meters

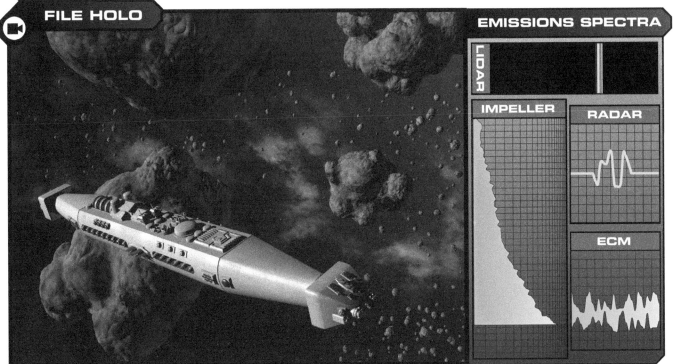

FILE HOLO

EMISSIONS SPECTRA

LIDAR

IMPELLER

RADAR

ECM

BRILLIANCE-CLASS LIGHT CRUISER

Ships in Class
Brilliance, Glimmer, Radiance, Solar Flare, Sunspot

Estimated Service Dates
1832-1901 P.D.

Specification
Mass: 120,000 tons
Length: 431 m
Beam: 45 m
Draught: 34 m
Acceleration: 518.1 G
Crew: 476 (45 Officers, 406 Enlisted, 25 Marines)
Power:
  2 RF/6 Dampierre 1 Fusion Reactors
Electronics
  AG-21(b) Gravitic Detection Array
  AR-22 Phased Radar Array
  AL-20(d) Lidar Arrayy
  SLCF-15 12-channel Fire Control System
  SDCC-15 12-channel Defensive Coordination and Control System
  ARBB-13 Electronic Countermeasures
Armament:
  12 LME-2 Missile Tubes
  4 L/72 Anti-Ship Lasers
  20 L/63 Anti-Ship Lasers
  12 LMC-8(b) Counter Missile Tubes
  8 P/16x2(a) Laser Clusters
Magazines
  156 E9 Impeller Drive Missiles
  408 C2 Counter Missiles
  8 LAD-24 Tethered ECM Decoys
Small Craft:
  3 D.435 *Ouragan*-class Pinnaces
  2 DB.100 *Mercure*-class Cutters

Design and Construction
The *Brilliance*-class light cruiser is one of the oldest cruiser designs still in service. Most commonly seen in the employ of various second rate navies, a few of these units remain in the service of the People's Republic.

When it was originally produced, the *Brilliance* was an effective platform. Before the introduction of laser head missiles with long standoff ranges, its heavy energy armament and adequate (for the period) anti-missile defenses let it close the range quickly and batter an opponent into submission.

While the class has been extensively refitted over the years, it has gradually fallen behind the tech curve, unable to compete with the realities of modern missile combat.

A more serious problem with the *Brilliance* class was their initial use of the L/72 Laser mounts. The L/72 was eventually replaced by the L/75 series (still in use today on many smaller ships) and most of the remaining L/72 stock was used in the first and second flight *Brilliances*. A serious glitch in the L/72's flux control software could cause the emitter assembly to fuse. Bad enough when this happened during routine testing, when the flaw occurred in combat, it resulted in casualties among the on-mount crews when the weapon was fired and destroyed itself.

Compounding the problem was the almost total lack of spares for the L/72 series emitters. After a number of accidents, the Bureau of Construction called in the remaining units, which underwent a rotating refit program, replacing them with the more reliable L/75 series, though some of the L/72 equipped ships have been sold to a number of Havenite "allies".

As many as two dozen *Brilliance*-class cruisers have been sold to the navies of smaller powers over the years, and at least a handful more have turned up in the hands of Silesian pirates. The People's Navy has had a longstanding tradition of selling off obsolete warships to help fund newer designs. With the start of the Manticoran Havenite war, this practice has slowed considerably, as even obsolete units are needed for picket duty on the frontiers.

Doctrinal Notes
As an obsolete close combat unit in a navy that is itself outclassed in electronics and penaids, the few remaining units of the *Brilliance*-class have been tucked away well behind the front, engaging in local system defense and pacification missions.

If one were to find itself in combat with anything larger than a destroyer, the captain's best hope would be to hold the wedge to the enemy and close to energy range as quickly as possible, in hopes of killing the opponent before being overwhelmed by incoming missiles.

Notable Units and Battles
While the People's Republic has usually been rather careful in choosing which "allied nations" it will sell hardware, it was not unheard of to find castoff Havenite units in the system defense forces of Haven's early conquests. It is rare, however, to find units of the exact same class on opposite sides of a battle. In 1886, the Maastricht system, which had already received several obsolete units, including three *Brilliance*-class light cruisers and two *Durandal*-class destroyers, was due to receive an additional transfer of two *Brilliance's* in addition to enough spares and ammunition to supply their system defense force for the foreseeable future. The second shipment was a trap, the two *Brilliance's* were accompanied by two *Trumball*-class Q-ships.

Unknown to the attackers, the Maastricht navy had been running a tracking exercise on their ships for training purposes. What should have been a one-sided surprise turned around when the tracking ships saw the *Trumballs* blow their panels, and the resulting engagement was devastating for both sides. The Maastricht navy was completely destroyed in the brief, savage exchange of fire, but one of the *Trumballs* and both *Brilliances* were severely damaged as well.

BRILLIANCE - TECHNICAL READOUT

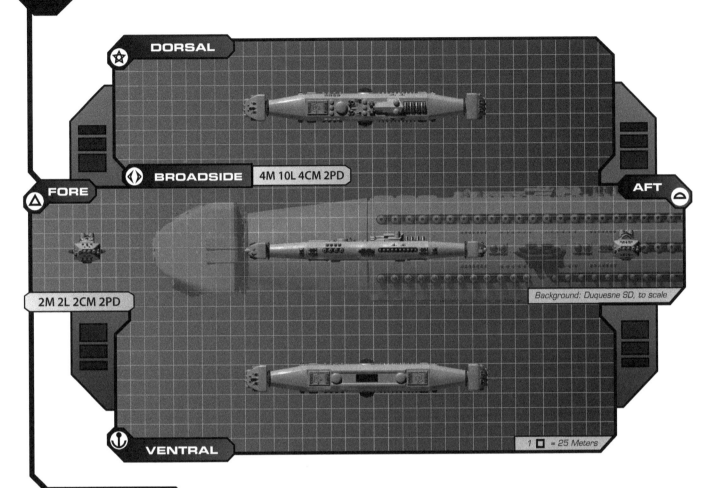

DORSAL

BROADSIDE 4M 10L 4CM 2PD

FORE

AFT

2M 2L 2CM 2PD

Background: Duquesne SD, to scale

VENTRAL

1 ☐ = 25 Meters

FILE HOLO

EMISSIONS SPECTRA

LIDAR

IMPELLER

RADAR

ECM

DESFORGE-CLASS DESTROYER

Ships in Class
Alcazar, Auphan, Baudin, Bouvet, Bruat, Courbet, Decrès, Desforge, Duperré, Hamelin, Kersaint, Linois, Morillot, Muselier, Dainville, Picquet, Requin, Roussin, Toulouse

Estimated Service Life
1887 to 1964 PD

Specification
Mass: 95,750 tons
Length: 393 m
Beam: 46 m
Draught: 27 m
Acceleration: 519.2 G
Crew: 435 (65 Officers, 370 Enlisted)
Power:
  2 RF/6 Dampierre 4 Fusion Reactors
Electronics
  AG-25(a) AG-25 Gravitic Detection Array
  AR-26 Phased Radar Array
  AL-26(a) Lidar Array
  SLCF-19 18x14-channel Distributed Control System
  ARBB-22 Electronic Countermeasures
Armament:
  12 LME-3(d) Missile Tubes
  2 L/75 Anti-Ship Lasers
  6 L/66 Anti-Ship Lasers
  10 LMC-8(g) Counter Missile Tubes
  8 P/16x3 Laser Clusters
Magazines:
  156 E14 Impeller Drive Missiles
  360 C2 Counter Missiles
  6 LAD-24 Tethered ECM Decoys
Small Craft:
  3 DB.100 *Mercure*-class Cutters
  2 D.435 *Ouragan*-class Pinnaces

Design and Construction
The *Desforge*-class of destroyer is a contemporary of the *Bastogne*-class, and was designed as a "balanced" destroyer, with a heavier defensive suite and lighter broadside. In particular, it was mandated into production by Legislaturalist political pressure, and only begrudgingly accepted over the objections of the People's Navy. In spite of the overly political nature of its creation, it appears to have been the first Naval design in living memory to actually come in under budget in both the design trials and series production.

The *Desforge*-class suffers from being the odd ship out in Havenite doctrinal usage, having a reduced throw weight compared to what doctrine demands. In a navy of specialist units, the *Desforge's* attempt to be "good enough" for multi-mission roles has made it less than favored in some circles.

Even with the opposition of the Navy, the *Desforge* is being built in large series runs—not as large as the more conventional *Bastogne*, but large enough to be a significant portion of the PN's destroyer inventory. As much as the admirals despise it as a screening unit, the accountants love its low cost and manpower requirements. Viewed without the blinders of the "win at the first salvo" doctrine, the *Desforge* is a capable ship.

Doctrinal Notes
Doctrinally, the *Desforge* is best used as a screening unit and scout; it has fairly long legs for a ship its size, and its defensive suite lets it survive encounters with enemy units when on picket duty. It also has fairly high armor for a ship of its rate, furthering survivability.

Most admirals who have *Desforges* assigned to them attempt to trade them for *Bastognes* if they have the political pull to do so, and send them on as convoy escorts and scouts if they can't get rid of them for something more capable.

Notable Units and Engagements
Commodore Carol Williamson, in command of TU 32, had a squadron of *Desforges* handed to her by her superior; ostensibly to use them as a screening unit to her cruiser division. When Manticoran forces hit her system to disrupt Havenite logistics in the early phases of the war, she separated her *Desforges* to escort supply freighters safely past the hyper limit, and threw her cruisers and light cruisers into the teeth of the Manticoran attackers. The resulting battle split into two parts - the Manticoran destroyers, and one *Warrior*-class heavy cruiser pursued the *Desforges* and freighters to the hyper limit, while the *Prince Consorts* and *Star Knights* drew out Williamson's heavier units into a tangential thrust against orbital facilities.

In the resulting battle, most of Williamson's heavy forces were destroyed, with two units surrendering, though they did bloody the Manticoran's nose in the process. The *Desforges*, organized as a screen around the freighters, managed to escort their charges to the hyper limit.

DESFORGE - TECHNICAL READOUT

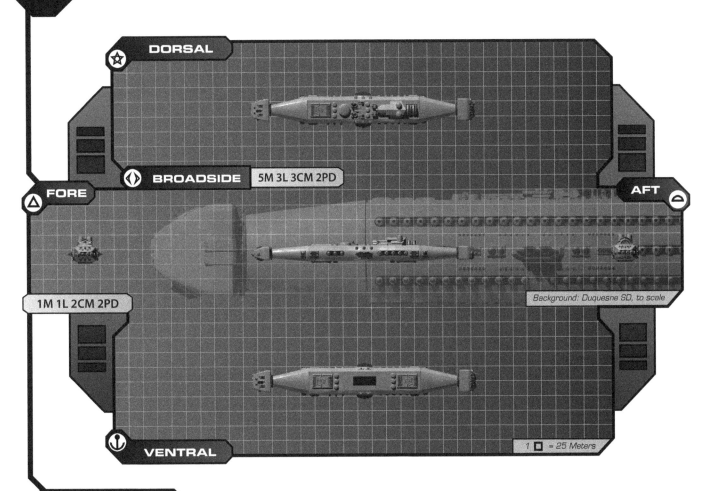

DORSAL

BROADSIDE | 5M 3L 3CM 2PD

FORE

AFT

Background: Duquesne SD, to scale

1M 1L 2CM 2PD

VENTRAL

1 ☐ = 25 Meters

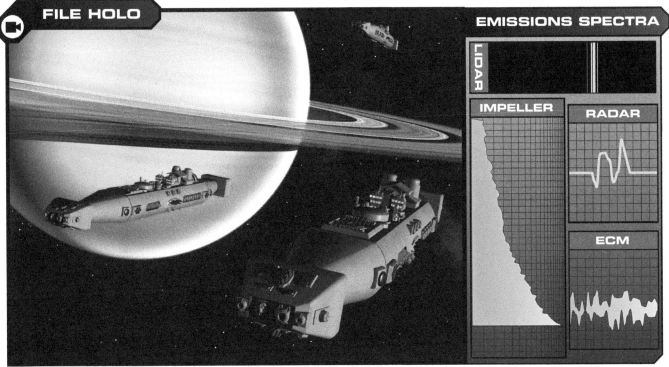

FILE HOLO

EMISSIONS SPECTRA

LIDAR

IMPELLER

RADAR

ECM

BASTOGNE-CLASS DESTROYER

Ships in Class
Arlon, Bastogne, Breslau, Bruges, Busko, Charleroi, Gorzow, Jaroslaw, Kessler, Krakow, Leuven, Liege, Lubin, Malbork, Poznan, Suwalki, Torun, Toulon, Tournai

Service Life
1883 to 1946 PD

Specification
Mass: 88,500 tons
Length: 383 m
Beam: 45 m
Draught: 26 m
Acceleration: 519.6 G
Crew: 417 (63 Officers, 354 Enlisted)
Power:
  2 RF/6 Dampierre 4 Fusion Reactors
Electronics
  AG-25 Gravitic Detection Array
  AR-26 Phased Radar Array
  AL-26(a) Lidar Array
  SLCF-19 18x8-channel Distributed Control System
  ARBB-22 Electronic Countermeasures
Armament:
  18 LME-3(c) Missile Tubes
  4 L/75 Anti-Ship Lasers
  4 L/66 Anti-Ship Lasers
  8 LMC-8(g) Counter Missile Tubes
  8 P/16x3 Laser Clusters
Magazines
  162 E14 Impeller Drive Missiles
  216 C2 Counter Missiles
  4 LAD-24 Tethered ECM Decoys
Small Craft:
  1 D.450 *Ouragan*-class Pinnace
  4 DB.100 *Mercure*-class Cutters

Design and Construction
The *Bastogne*-class destroyer is the product of a design philosophy prevalent in the pre-war People's Navy. Faced with a large number of systems to be garrisoned, the Office of Planning needed copious numbers of light combatants for perimeter security forces. The *Bastogne* is one of those designs.

The *Bastogne* class has been derided by some within the People's Navy as a "LAC with a gland condition and hyper capability". It has neither the magazine space nor the defenses to survive sustained combat operations, but is intended to pack in the maximum possible broadside capability at the expense of a credible energy weapon deterrence, magazine space and defenses. It mounts the quick-firing but unreliable LME-3(c) launchers.

The *Bastogne's* defenses are sub-par across the spectrum. The magazine stowage proportions of counter-missiles to ship-killers is very low, especially in light of the ship's extremely light energy armament, with a corresponding reduction in point defense efficiency. These shortcomings have been exacerbated by the gap between Manticoran and Havenite electronics since the start of the war.

The poor quality of its defenses and short endurance force the *Bastogne* out of two of the most common roles for a destroyer. With an endurance far shorter than most of its contemporaries and an unbalanced weapons fit heavy on offensive power, it is poorly suited for escort duties and the lack of marines make it unsuited to anti-piracy operations. Most *Bastognes* are found as advanced screens for the wall of battle, where its role is to get its missiles off quickly before it is destroyed, a fact that does not endear it to its crews.

As a small concession to its reduced energy armament, the *Bastogne* mounts heavier beam weapons than are normally seen on a ship of its size. The difference is minimal, given the single laser in each broadside.

Doctrinal Notes
With a weapon fit overbalanced towards offense, and an almost suicidal shortage of defenses, the *Bastogne*-class is used for high speed drive by passes, salvoing missiles and running as quickly as possible. A secondary use of the *Bastognes* is as a lure on a raiding mission, their task to pull enemy units into dispersed hunter/seeker patterns to make them vulnerable to defeat in detail.

Its best tactic in combat is to close quickly to optimal missile range, getting the maximum use out of its heavy broadside, then retreat and hope the enemy's battle damage has rendered it unable or unwilling to pursue. Its missile-heavy design can also be a liability at close ranges, where shorter tracking time and response loops favor ships that are fast on the helm with heavy beam armaments.

One recent (and unorthodox) variant on standard doctrine involves operating *Bastognes* and *Conquerors* in divisional strength, stationed right on the hyper limit on a least-time course along the axis of threat. If the timing is right, the missile-heavy ships are well positioned to intercept and severely damage the enemy's lead units as they come out of hyper. It is a cold, calculated move, balancing the probable loss of the entire division against the damage they can inflict on the opposing force's screen before they are destroyed.

Notable Units and Battles
Some proposals have been put forth to modernize the remainder of the *Bastognes* still in service. PNS *Bruges* was chosen as a test platform, replacing three missile tubes in each broadside with lasers and spreading the existing magazines among the remaining launchers. While a much more survivable design, both in terms of its sustained rate of fire and antimissile defenses, the cost was too high to warrant a complete refit for the remaining units.

BASTOGNE - TECHNICAL READOUT

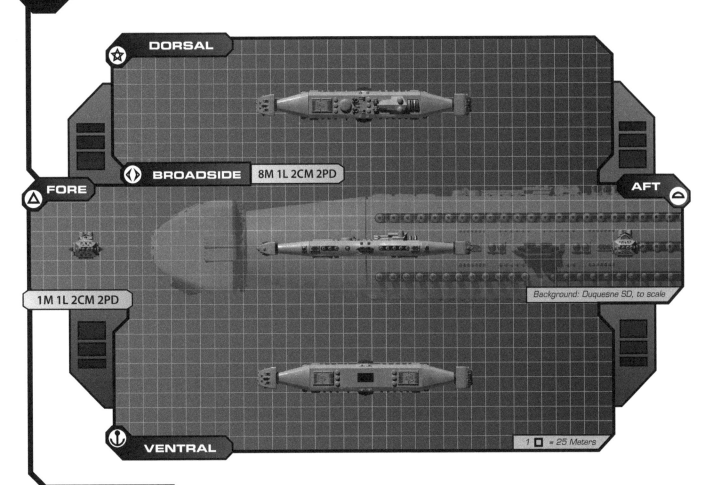

DORSAL

BROADSIDE 8M 1L 2CM 2PD

FORE

AFT

1M 1L 2CM 2PD

Background: Duquesne SD, to scale

VENTRAL

1 ☐ = 25 Meters

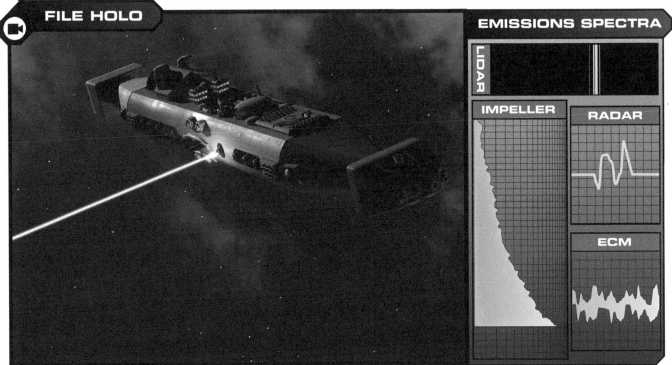

FILE HOLO

EMISSIONS SPECTRA

LIDAR

IMPELLER

RADAR

ECM

PROGRAM 13 CLASS LIGHT ATTACK CRAFT

Estimated Service Life
1835 PD to 1912 PD

Specification
Mass: 10,250 tons
Length: 134 m
Beam: 22 m
Draught: 21 m
Acceleration: 409.6 G
Crew: 25 (4 Officers, 21 Enlisted)
Power:
  1 RF/2 Bugey 1 Fusion Reactor
Electronics
  AG-31(a) Gravitic Detection Array
  AR-32 Phased Radar Array
  AL-30(d) Lidar Array
  SLCF-16 8-channel Fire Control System
  ARBB-14 Electronic Countermeasures
Armament:
  LMB-1(a) Modular Launch System
  2 L/21 Lasers
  6 P/12x2 Laser Clusters
Ordnance:
  32 B10 Impeller Drive Missiles

Design and Development
The *Program 13* class LAC is an evolutionary design in Havenite system defense craft, replacing the earlier *Guêpe*-class nearly seventy years ago. Most of the changes were fairly minor - upgrading components to systems currently in production, taking advantages in minor improvements in efficiency to shift passageways to make the hull easier to navigate. Even with these changes, the LACs lack the internal volume devoted to accessways to make long term maintenance worthwhile. LACs are deployed for long stretches of relatively hard use, and after a couple of decades, get retired or rotated to less important systems as they wear out.

Havenite *Program 13* class LACs use box launchers to maximize throw weight, and the *Program-13* class, starting with the C-series upgrades, uses an 8 missile box launcher, rather than the more conventional 6-tube launcher used in Silesian and Manticoran service. The *Program 13* series carries two P/12x2 Laser Clusters in each broadside, and a P/12x2 and L/21 Laser in both the bow and stern for defensive firepower. Like most Havenite vessels, the laser has additional tracking equipment to facilitate defensive use.

Program 13 LACs were built in enormous quantity in the last five decades as the DuQuesne Expansion progressed. Individual units only have numbers, and the "Program Number" designation is a holdover from the design study; the class itself never received a formal name. While some money has been spent on developing upgrades to the existing *Program 13*s, the general consensus is that there are too many of them in service, spread too far apart, to make upgrading them cost effective.

The recommendations of the Office of Naval Construction are to push forward on the E-series modifications for the *Program 13s* and replace existing craft on a squadron-for-squadron basis as they wear out.

Doctrinal Notes
Doctrinally, *Program 13s* fulfill customs patrol and SAR roles in friendly systems. In systems that have been recently conquered, they are deployed on a *Raskin*-class orbital facility in near orbit to planets. The *Raskin* serves as a base, LAC tender, and orbital port facility for trade regulation; its LAC squadrons are used for orbital interdiction and suppression roles. The *Program-13's* acceleration, while pitiful compared to a real warship, is sufficient for interdiction of orbital space, and PD clusters capable of engaging laser heads at 30,000 km are capable of shooting down atmospheric craft from 250 km high orbits.

PROGRAM 13 - TECHNICAL READOUT

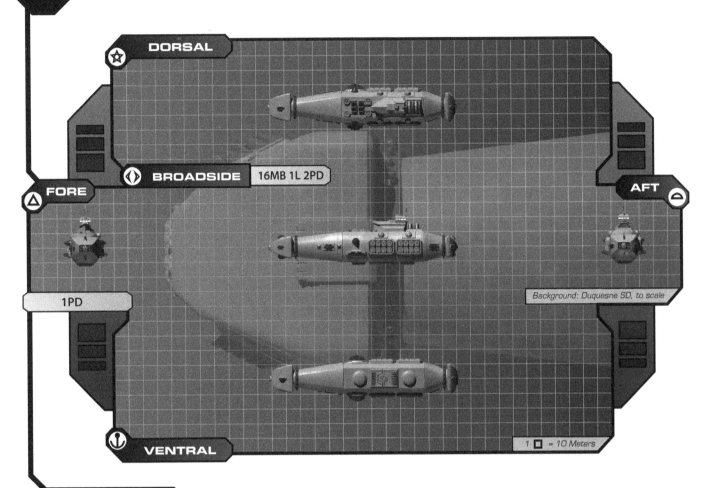

DORSAL

BROADSIDE 16MB 1L 2PD

FORE

AFT

1PD

Background: Duquesne SD, to scale

VENTRAL

1 □ = 10 Meters

FILE HOLO

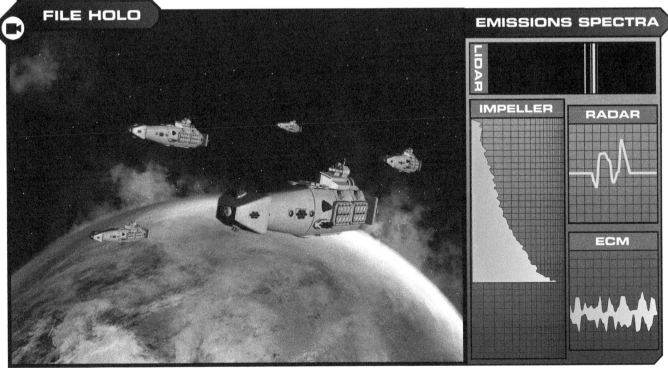

EMISSIONS SPECTRA

LIDAR

IMPELLER

RADAR

ECM

ASTRA-CLASS ARMED MERCHANT CRUISER

Ships in Class
Astra, Cygni, Sirius, Procyon

Expected Service Life
1897-1946 PD

Specification
Mass: 7,579,500 tons
Length: 1,213 m
Beam: 200 m
Draught: 194 m
Accelerati on: 412.3 G
Crew: 1498 (150 Officers, 1348 Enlisted)
Power:
  2 RF/5 Marrone 2 Fusion Reactors
Electronics
  AG-15 Gravitic Detection Array
  AR-92 "Starfinder" Navigation Radar
  AR-18(a) Phased Radar Array
  AL-13 Lidar Array
  SLCF-19(a) 68x42channel Distributed Control System
  ARBB-23 Electronic Countermeasures
Armament:
  52 LMF-5(d) Missile Tubes
  24 G/140 Grasers
  36 LMC-8(g) Counter Missile Tubes
  28 P/18x6 Anti-Missile Lasers
Magazines
  6240 F17 Impeller Drive Missiles
  12960 C2 Counter Missiles
  12 LAD-5(c) Tethered ECM Decoys
Small Craft:
  6 DB.100 *Mercure*-class Cutters
  2 D.435 *Ouragan*-class Pinnaces
  2 C.160 *Transall*-class Cargo Shuttles
Cargo: 4,896,500 tons

Design and Construction
The *Astra*-class armed merchant raider is a new design based on lessons learned from the older *Trumball*-class. Units of this class were built in the Lovat yards, which have experience building armed auxiliary units. The People's Republic kept reasonable operational security on their construction by building them in mixed series with conventional freighters.

The *Astra*-class was never especially numerous, though exact quantities are unknown, and the People's Republic of Haven has at various times given directly contradictory answers about the existance of the class, number in service, whether any more are bing built, or even stating the entire class is a fabrication of a smear campaign. The external appearance is identical to that of the *Astra*-class bulk freighter, a successful design found throughout the People's Merchant Service. Internally, however, the *Astra* is built more like a warship than a merchant.

A second reactor is buried deep in the core, though the ship runs on its single merchant grade reactor during routine operations to mimic the emissions signature of its unarmed cousin.

Doctrinal Notes
Unlike the *Trumbull*-class, which was used primarily as a first strike unit and in commerce raiding, the *Astra*-class is intended to stay on station acting out its role as just another merchant for longer periods. While many of its hatches are merely to disguise its true origin, it does retain significant cargo capacity, including two cargo shuttles.

The concealment options on the *Astra* class are numerous, including drive nodes on a powered "ram", and blow-away panels over the military-grade gravitic and speed-of-light sensors. Spare weapon and sensor-concealment panels are carried aboard though mounting them is a time and labor intensive process.

In combat, the *Astra* has sluggish handling, due to the compromises in the design made for concealment. Her acceleration is quite impressive for an armed merchant vessel, at 400+ Gs. With a throw weight comparable to a battlecruiser, her magazine levels rival those of a superdreadnought.

Notable Units and Battles
The only *Astra*-class to see combat was PNS *Sirius*. In 1900 P.D. *Sirius* was chased down and destroyed by the Manticoran light cruiser HMS *Fearless*. The Royal Manticoran Navy has refused to release any details of the battle, but (assuming the claims of an *Astra* being destroyed are accurate), the complete destruction of a seven and a half eight million ton Q-ship at the hands of an eighty-eight thousand ton light cruiser is the subject of considerable wardroom debate.

ASTRA - TECHNICAL READOUT

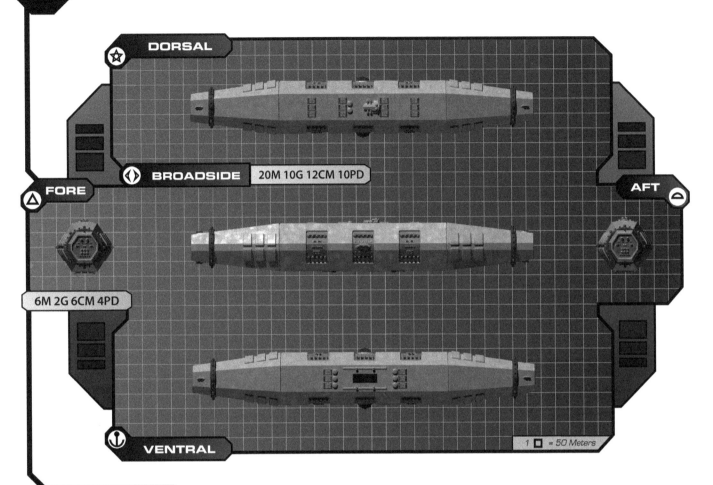

DORSAL

BROADSIDE 20M 10G 12CM 10PD

FORE

AFT

6M 2G 6CM 4PD

VENTRAL

1 □ = 50 Meters

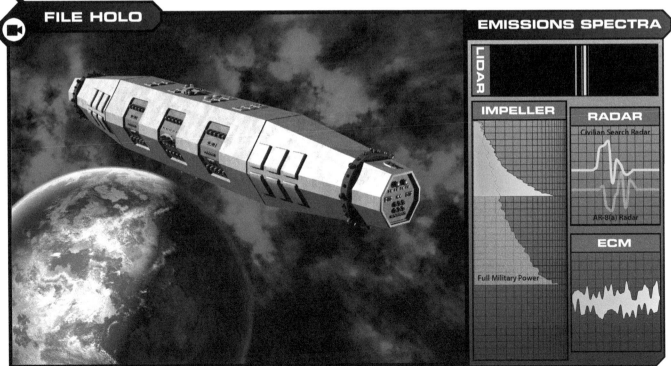

FILE HOLO

EMISSIONS SPECTRA

LIDAR

IMPELLER

Full Military Power

RADAR

Civilian Search Radar

AR-8(a) Radar

ECM

ROUGHNECK-CLASS FAST ATTACK TRANSPORT

Ships in Class
Foudre, Leatherneck, Roughneck, Siroco

Estimated Service Dates
1846 to 1964 PD

Specification
Mass: 4,545,250 tons
Length: 1,021 m
Beam: 170 m
Draught: 158 m
Acceleration: 207.0 G
Crew: 21000 (38 Officers, 212 Enlisted, 20750 Marines)
Power:
  2 RF/5 Chinon 2 Fusion Reactors
Electronics
  AG-3 Gravitic Detection Array
  AR-3 Phased Radar Array
  SLCF-17(c) 0x24-channel Distributed Control System
  ARBB-17 Electronic Countermeasures
Armament:
  24 LMC-8(d) Counter Missile Tubes
  36 P/16x5 Laser Clusters
  720 C2 Counter Missiles
  6 LAD-5(c) Tethered ECM Decoys
Small Craft:
  2 D.450 *Ouragan*-class Pinnaces
  84 DR.41 *Razzia*-class Assault Shuttles
Cargo: 662,000 tons

Design and Construction
The *Roughneck*-class transport is purpose built for planetary invasion. Capable of carrying a fully equipped People's Navy Marine Division with all support personnel and heavy equipment, the *Roughneck* also provides orbital command and control facilities and secure hospital facilities, carrying an extra 5,000 troops beyond the full Division load for support, administration, and military police duties, and after an assault drop, roughly 1,000 Marine berths can be readily converted into brigs for prisoner retention and interrogation with 24 hours of labor.

The *Roughneck* has three conventional boat bays, with the center bay carrying a quartet of pinnaces. The forward and aft bays hold

6 *Razzia*-class assault shuttles. Unlike a conventional combatant, the upper decks are sliced through with 6 more transverse boat bays, running from port to starboard. Each of those bays holds a dozen additional *Razzias*, giving a total drop capacity of 84 assault shuttles. Each bay has a full ordnance handling unit and repair team, and the *Roughneck* can deploy the entire Division from its organic assault shuttles. Properly planned, the shuttles can launch at the rate of two per bay per minute, and the entire launch plan can be done in under 15 minutes.

This voluminous drop capability allows the *Roughneck* to deploy the full strength division in one exo-atmospheric interface operation, though the 5,000 support troops require a second run from the pinnaces. This second run presumes that a secure planetary landing position will have been established by the first wave.

In addition to her Marine complement, the *Roughnecks* have a full naval crew—indeed, nearly 1,000 Naval personnel are tied into small craft piloting and support duties.

The greatest limit on the *Roughneck* is its cargo capacity; the cargo bays in the *Roughneck* are interstitial, and the compromises made into the ship's structure for the transverse launch bays mean that the primary cargo entry point has to be the forward and aft bays. In an emergency, the *Roughneck* can carry cargo and ordnance in the transverse bays, but the cargo is only nominally secured, and there is no effective way to transfer it to ship's stores—the airlocks are smaller to preserve structural strength. This limitation has caused requests for a larger transport, one capable of transporting and supporting a Marine Division for up to a year onboard from organic cargo capabilities and with improved cargo handling equipment; in particular, this would allow for embarkation of more materiel-intensive People's Army units.

Doctrinal Notes
The *Roughnecks* have no offensive weaponry at all, and have the sidewalls and defensive suite of a heavy cruiser or older battlecruiser, in spite of massing as much as a battleship. Operationally, the People's Navy does its level best to ensure that *Roughnecks* never see combat in space; the aim is to send *Roughnecks* in to planets after the People's Navy has swatted aside any space-based defenders.

ROUGHNECK - TECHNICAL READOUT

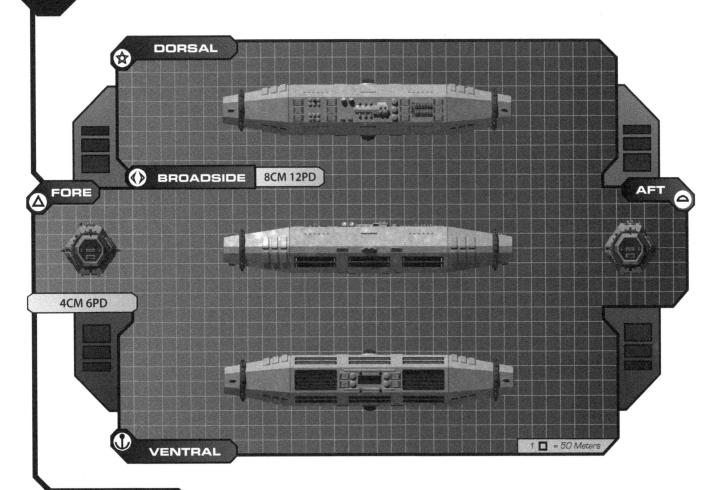

DORSAL

BROADSIDE 8CM 12PD

FORE

AFT

4CM 6PD

1 □ = 50 Meters

VENTRAL

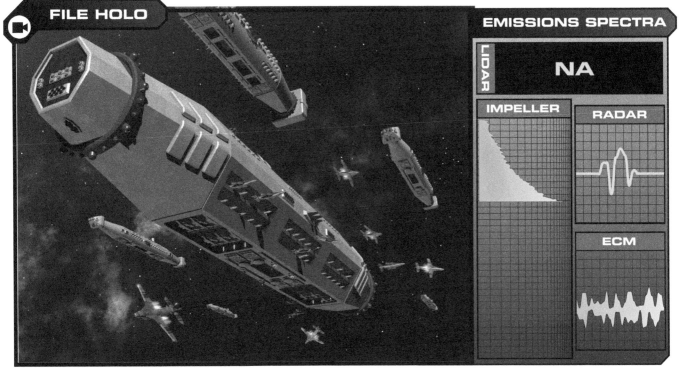

FILE HOLO

EMISSIONS SPECTRA

LIDAR NA

IMPELLER

RADAR

ECM

FACTEUR-CLASS COURIER BOAT

Ships in Class
As with many smaller types of auxiliaries and civilian vessels, courier boats are not assigned names, only hull numbers. The *Facteur*-class is assigned the prefix "49" in the national registry.

Estimated Service Dates
1872 to 1985 PD

Specification
Mass: 38,000 tons
Length: 294 m
Beam: 31 m
Draught: 24 m
Acceleration: 535.7 G
Crew: 30 (7 Officers, 22 Enlisted, 6 Passengers)
Power:
1 RF/3 BdG 2 Fusion Reactor
Electronics
AG-13 Gravitic Detection Array
"Starfinder" Navigation Radar
Small Craft:
1 Cutter (design varies)

Design and Construction
The *Facteur*-class courier boat is representative of several different classes of government-owned courier boats in the People's Republic. The wide astrographical expanse of the People's Republic requires a network of ships that can transit carrying routine, commercial and official message traffic. Originally run by competing private companies, as the Legislaturalist regime ossified, more of them were turned into sector and regional monopolies held by prominent families. In the 1880s, nepotism and corruption in the monopolies allowed news of a secessionist movement in Morell to be lost completely, which let them acquire battlecruisers and attempt to break free of the People's Republic. The political fallout caused several prominent families to be publicly stripped of their holdings, and the courier boat system was nationalized for the security of the Republic.

Now, all courier vessels are nominally staffed with Naval crews, even those belonging to the Diplomatic Corps and those tasked with carrying routine message traffic of civil and civilian nature. Having gotten that part of the Republic's budget, the Navy is dead set on keeping it, even when Naval standards require larger crews than are strictly necessary for the ships operations.

Ships like the *Facteur*-class are fairly similar in their operations - they are physically the smallest ships that can mount a hyper generator and a pair of Warshawski sails. Most have compensators that are close to, or exceed, military specifications for acceleration rates; indeed, the contractors trying to sell the Republic new courier boats host regattas and "yacht races" to showcase their newest compensator improvements, and the impeller nodes are larger than normal for their capacity to allow for ease of maintenance and long term operations.

The courier boat is completely unarmed, lacking in even countermissile or point defense arrays. To save mass and volume, the only ranging and targeting equipment the ships have are docking radars, though their gravitics arrays are extensive, particularly their forward and aft Warshawkis, a critial feature for a ship that spends much of its time in the higher hyper bands and more turbulent grav waves.

The message traffic on a *Facteur* is stored in a secure database that the crew does not have access to, other than routing codes for delivery; this database is designed to destroy itself if tampered with The courier boats operated by the People's Navy for the Diplomatic Corps have berths for diplomatic personnel, and limited cargo capacities. This space can be re-purposed for carrying a squad of commando or special forces operatives at need.

Doctrinal Notes
The *Facteur* and similar classes of vessel are meant to avoid combat at all costs; routine scheduling of transits and message traffic are set up in ways such that a courier boat that fails to report is immediately noticed, and a Naval unit is sent out to investigate.

FACTEUR - TECHNICAL READOUT

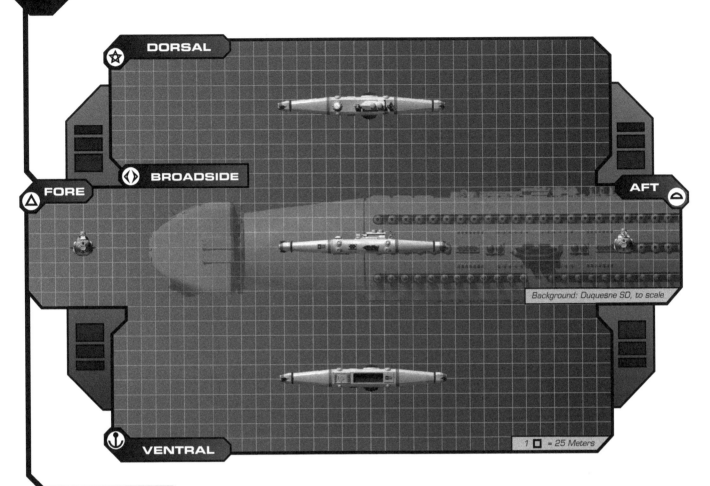

DORSAL

BROADSIDE

FORE

AFT

Background: Duquesne SD, to scale

VENTRAL

1 ☐ = 25 Meters

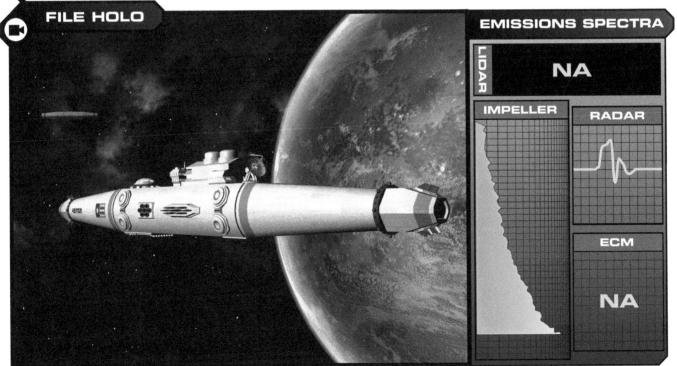

FILE HOLO

EMISSIONS SPECTRA

LIDAR

NA

IMPELLER

RADAR

ECM

NA

PEOPLE'S MARINE CORPS

The People's Marine Corps is an odd hybrid of independence and subordination to the People's Navy. It has, since the founding of the Republic of Haven, been a separate branch of the Armed Services, having its own "slots" of flag rank officers at the Octagon. However, in deployment, the People's Marine Corps acts subordinate to the People's Navy.

The PMCs has had good fortune in getting solid and dependable personnel, even from the Dolist ranks. PMC boot camps are known to be brutally rigorous, and their recruiting ads use that as a selling point - only the best of the best can become People's Marines. Those that make it through have a high esprit de corps and tend to be self selected for personal initiative, bravery bordering on the suicidal, or both. The PMC knew before the Manticoran war that it had a technological disparity to overcome, just from looking at Solarian League equipment. Rather than grumble to the House of Legislators for equipment that would take decades to develop and deploy and that would likely never arrive due to budgetary overrides for Naval spending, the PMC made a concerted effort to overcome the disparity with leadership, morale and élan. This has caused some derision of the crispness that the Marines spend on ceremonials, particularly from junior Naval officers who can't get that kind of performance out of their enlisted personnel, but the results are quite noticeable. While Haven has the capability to overwhelm with sheer numbers and raw manpower, the PMC

begrudges spending the lives of its Marines like water, and will attempt to adapt, survive and overcome. Those who have faced the PMC in ground action don't look forward to doing it twice.

The Marines have done a better job of hanging onto long-term noncoms than the Navy, and they have always emphasized that aspect of their force structure. The Marines work hard to maintain flexibility and initiative at the junior officer, with extensive training in the service academy and OCS to overcome the Havenite educational system.

The Marines rely on the partnership between their company and platoon officers and senior, long-service noncoms. Ranks above Major are virtually closed to anyone without Legislaturalist ties. There is a strong tradition of mustangs in the PMC, and approximately 15% of all officers in the Marine Corps Academy are senior NCOs who bucked for the OCS exams and passed. Most mustangs hit a glass "glass ceiling" at Captain or Major, since they have difficulty getting onto an Intel or Staff billet.

Operationally, the PMC has to fight a certain degree of inertia and "hidebound" thinking, brought on by the closure of high ranks to Marines with inadequate political capital, and the inertia of half a century of continued success.

PMC ORGANIZATION - FROM THE GROUND UP

A rifle platoon consists of fifty marines (three rifle squads and a single support squad) led by a 1st Lieutenant, with a command section consisting of a staff sergeant, clerk and marine corpsman.

A PMC rifle squad consists of twelve marines led by a sergeant. The squad is split into two rifle sections of 3 riflemen led by a corporal and a 2-man tribarrel section also led by a corporal.

The support squad consists of ten marines, led by a sergeant. Two plasma rifle teams are each led by a corporal and a 3-man tribarrel team carrying the T19 medium tribarrel makes up the final section. In standard deployment, the Lieutenant moves with the support squad.

A heavy weapons squad consists of 3 crew served heavy weapons (heavy tribarrels, plasma cannon, automatic grenade launchers, SAM teams or mortars), and numbers 13 men (4 for each weapon, plus the command sergeant). Three heavy weapon squads make up one heavy weapon platoon, led by a 1st Lieutenant.

A rifle company consists of 160 marines. Three rifle platoons led by a Captain, with a command section consisting of a gunnery sergeant, three staff lieutenants, three clerks and two corpsmen.

A heavy weapons company is made up of three heavy weapon platoons, led by Captain. Command staff and layout of the platoons differs based on role, the most typical being two platoons of infantry support weapons and a single platoon of anti-air and anti-armor weapons. Weapons companies include a maintenance platoon to service the company's equipment.

A rifle battalion consists of three rifle companies and a single weapons company led by a Major or Lt. Colonel. Heavy weapons are concentrated at the battalion level and assigned accordingly, instead of being cross-attached at the company or platoon level. Shipboard doctrine is to cross-attach a weapons company fitted with battle armor as the assault component. The battalion is the largest PMC unit that ever gets permanently assigned to a warship.

A regiment consists of three battalions, while a brigade consists of three regiments and accompanying command staff. Both units are used as administrative units in ground assault divisions, but rarely function as independent units.

A division consists of three brigades (27 battalions total) and is the standard unit of transport for ground assault operations.

PMC ORGANIZATION

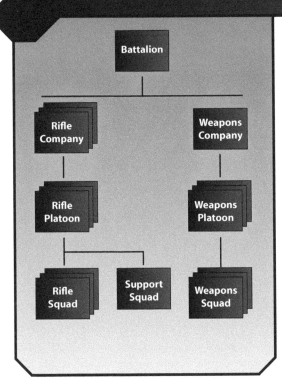

Battalion

Rifle Company

Weapons Company

Rifle Platoon

Weapons Platoon

Rifle Squad

Support Squad

Weapons Squad

STANDARD DROP CONFIGURATION

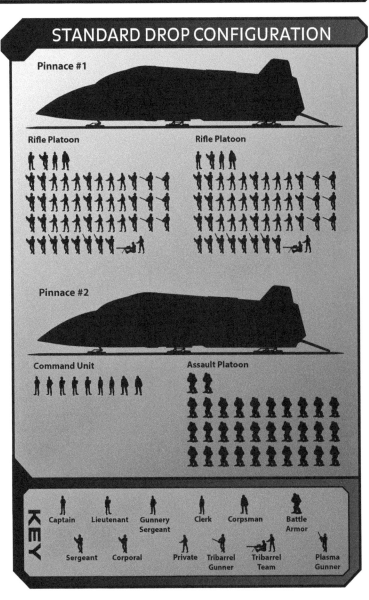

Pinnace #1

Rifle Platoon

Rifle Platoon

Pinnace #2

Command Unit

Assault Platoon

KEY

Captain | Lieutenant | Gunnery Sergeant | Clerk | Corpsman | Battle Armor

Sergeant | Corporal | Private | Tribarrel Gunner | Tribarrel Team | Plasma Gunner

PMC EMBLEM

PMC RIFLE PLATOON

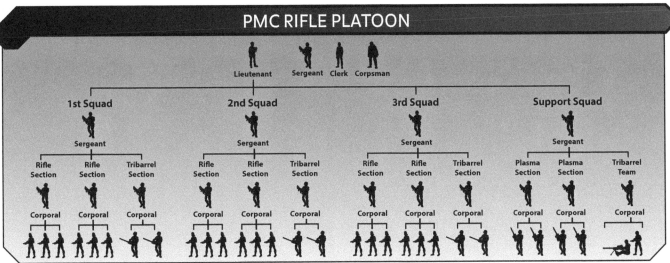

Lieutenant   Sergeant   Clerk   Corpsman

1st Squad | 2nd Squad | 3rd Squad | Support Squad

Sergeant | Sergeant | Sergeant | Sergeant

Rifle Section | Rifle Section | Tribarrel Section | Rifle Section | Rifle Section | Tribarrel Section | Rifle Section | Rifle Section | Tribarrel Section | Plasma Section | Plasma Section | Tribarrel Team

Corporal | Corporal | Corporal | Corporal | Corporal | Corporal | Corporal | Corporal | Corporal | Corporal | Corporal | Corporal

OFFICER'S UNDRESS UNIFORM

The People's Marine Corps officer's dress uniform shares features with the uniform of the People's Navy. The jacket is brown with green trim and black bands at the cuffs, worn over a green undertunic. The collar insignia is identical to that of the navy. Shoulderboards are not worn, but the crossed rifles of the Corps and a duplicate of the collar insignia are worn on the strap.

The working uniform removes the brown coat, and just uses the bloused green undertunic as a working garment. The tunic is unadorned, and lacks the soft "shoulderboards" used by the Naval undress tunic. It seals up the front with a wraparound collar and

displays an embroidered name badge above the left pocket, with the rank insignia on the collar.

The trousers are standard navy grey with green striping. Cuffs are loose fit over high topped black boots. An optional black gunbelt with silver buckle can be worn over the jacket.

The cap is the same high peaked style as worn by the People's Navy, with the symbol of the People's Republic on the front flash. The body of the cap is brown with green trim, matching the tunic.

MARINE SKINSUIT

The C9A skinsuit is an armored version of the standard C9 naval skinsuit. Designed for use in shipboard and hostile environment combat, the C9A replaces the natural protection of the skinsuit outer layer with a series of ceramic armor plates over the torso, spine, hips and shoulders. The helmet is significantly upgraded, with targeting and tracking systems, and combat endurance is extended with a heavier backpack life support system.

Mobility is critical in close combat of boarding actions, and the C9A's armor plating is carefully placed to minimize its impact on the flexibility and "sprint" capabilities of the person wearing it. The C9A lacks strength augmentation, however. This makes it much more strenuous to climb ladders in the rig under a standard gravity, and a person is not as acrobatic or nimble as one in a standard C9 skinsuit. The flexible parts of the armor are rated as small arms resistant, the armor plates are considered small arms "proof"; neither is rated against infantry combat main arms.

The C9A's thrusters are a significant improvement over those of the C9s, as the plates allow a somewhat more energetic exhaust, and the heavier backpack has a higher output system. The control interface, because of the greater mass, results in a tendency to oversteer; once this is compensated for, the C9A's thrusters allow for a finer degree of control. The thrust control computers handshake with the tactical computer and the backpack contains most of the computational assets and an extensive power reserve.

The tactical computer can accept feeds from all standard infantry weapons, and display weapon targeting information on the helmet HUD. The sockets for plugs are oversized, so that a person in vacuum suitable gloves can swap cables freely. It also houses an expanded communications suite for tactical coordination.

Critics of the C9A armored skinsuit complain that too little attention is given to long term habitability, particularly compared to the lighter and more comfortable C8 model that it replaces. The weight distribution of the C9, even without the armor plating that makes up the C9A, rests more heavily on the wearer's shoulders than the prior C8 did, which was weighted more along the waist, but gave a somewhat "potbellied" appearance to the wearer. One strong critique of the C9A versus the C9A is that the armor plating

has covered up almost all of the "handy points" – places where a wearer can attach a tool or attach a tether to keep something from drifting away in freefall. Likewise, the thigh plating has covered the cargo pockets that are part of the standard C9. Both the C9 and C9A have a more ergonomically designed set of helmet switches and water nozzle for drinking while the suit is worn.

Marines onboard PN starships don their C9A skinsuits when the ship goes to general quarters. Unlike the C9 naval variant, the C9A is not well suited to long periods locked into a shock frame, as the enlarged backpack restricts the ability of the wearer to twist at the waist, and for tall personnel, forces them to sit slightly hunched forward in a position that makes the lower back ache after an extended period of time. Despite such complaints, the C9A remains the standard in light armor protection for the People's Marines.

THRUSTER CONFIG

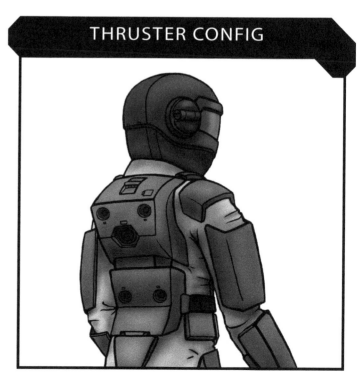

OFFICER'S UNIFORM AND SKINSUIT

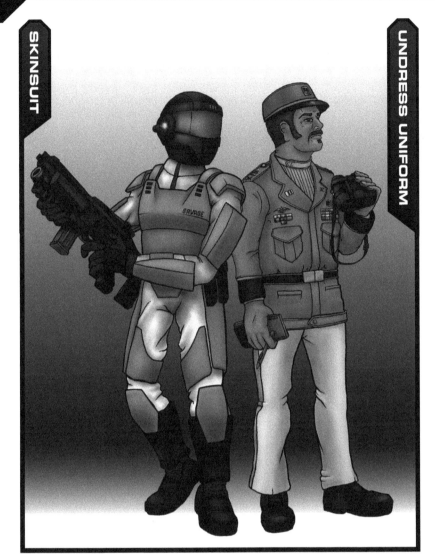

SKINSUIT

UNDRESS UNIFORM

COMBAT DROP PIN

STRAP BUTTON

STRAP PIN

INSIGNIA

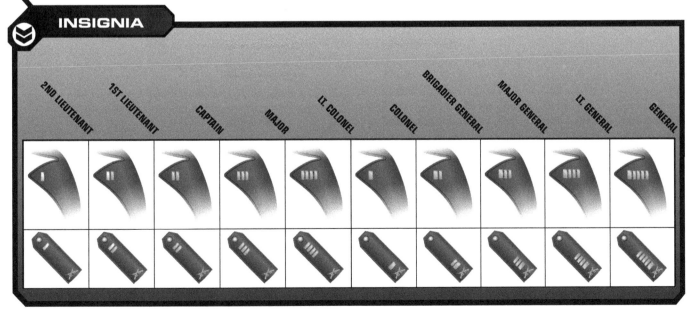

2ND LIEUTENANT	1ST LIEUTENANT	CAPTAIN	MAJOR	LT. COLONEL	COLONEL	BRIGADIER GENERAL	MAJOR GENERAL	LT. GENERAL	GENERAL

ENLISTED UNDRESS UNIFORM

The People's Marine Corps enlisted undress uniform is a brown, one-piece coverall similar in styling to that of the Navy. Unlike the Naval uniform, it does not have the color coded chest panel to denote departments. Cargo carriage is covered by pockets on the chest and waist, with cargo pockets suitable for carrying a tactical computer on the thighs. A pistol belt may be worn as required, dark brown with an unadorned buckle, though routine use of the pistol belt causes much grumbling, as it further enhances the practical difficulties of a single piece garment. The coveralls seal up the front, and the collar is unadorned on enlisted personnel.

The Marine boots differ from Naval footwear in that they're designed for greater comfort and durability. The cuff of the legs of the overall is tucked into the Marine boots.

Rating insignia is worn by Marines on both arms in green trimmed black. Just below the insignia is a crossed rifles patch. A nametag is worn on the upper edge of the left pocket. The same system of bezels are used to show time in grade on the name tag. Citing the possibility of detection in the field, the Marine Corps does not use RFID s in their personnel nametags. In practice, this is because the People's Marine Corps expects a higher standard of motivation and work ethic among its enlisted personnel, and has the traditions to make these expectations happen.

The cap is the same brown as the uniform and bears the crossed rifles of the People's Marines to the left of the center seam.

A6 BATTLE ARMOR

The A6 Battle Armor is the current powered armor combat suit in service with the People's Marines. The system has been in service for over twenty years and proven to be a reliable, effective system.

The A6 is composed of an inner bodysuit, custom fitted to the wearer, inside the armored shell. The outer shell is single piece construction, hinged at the waist for easier entry. The back panel is sealed for atmospheric integrity, and covered by a backplate, and then the backpack itself. Donning an A6 takes a standard crew of 2, though the racks in most starship installations (cheerfully referred to as "The Morgue") contain automated brackets to allow for a single user to climb into a suit.

The armor of the A6 is a combination of active matrix armor over critical areas with layers of myoflexible armor over the joints. The active matrix system consists of a high power EM field to disrupt plasma flow and layers of semiablative armorplast to dissipate and absorb energy and kinetic attacks. The joints are covered with a mesh of armor cells using low-power myomers for assisted flexibility.

The backpack houses the suit's power supply and primary thruster system. Power endurance varies by mission and usage levels, ranging from as little as two hours of intense combat to 40 hours in minimal drain. The backpack also houses the suit's electronic and active countermeasures, including a small multi purpose launcher for flares, chaff, communications and sensor drones.

The backpack has a backup power cell for emergency use, which can provide enough power to run the life support and slow assisted movement. In the case of complete loss of power or emergency egress, the user can trigger explosive bolts to break the backpack clear, and climb out. Standard survival gear is stored in a small compartment in the "groin", including a first aid kid, emergency rations and supplements and a M5 sidearm to sustain and protect the operator in a shirtsleeve planetary environment. Marines being marines, the jokes about what someone's packing between their legs are endemic, and generally considered good for morale.

The standard sensor package includes visual and IR sensors, passive Electronic Support Measures (ESM) gear and active targeting arrays. In addition, remote autonomous communication and sensor drones can feed into the suit's tactical network through wideband encrypted communications. The drones are launched from the multi-launcher in the backpack and have an operating endurance of 2 hours in countergrav mode. If emplaced as passive ground sensors, the drones can operate as remote listening posts for several days.

A matrix of visual/IR sensors on the outside of the armor suit feed into the threat detection and active camouflage systems. The refresh cycle on the active camouflage system is on the low side, allowing updates of the image projected on the surface of the armor about 4-5 times per second, making the system more useful in a static environment than a dynamic one.

The gauntlets of the A6 are heavily armored but poorly suited to fine manipulation. This renders the A6 unable to operate standard personnel equipment. A variety of standard infantry carried weapon systems have modifications for the A6, including a rugged outer shell and power and targeting feeds run through a wrist connection. The weapons that interface with the armor include the L49AB Pulse Rifle for low-intensity operations as well as the T17 Light Tribarrel, T19 Medium Tribarrel, and P21 Infantry Plasma Weapon.

For assault configuration, handheld versions of the crew served T36 Heavy Tribarrel and P13 Plasma Cannon can be carried, though the power drain of both of these weapons is considerable. Standard assault doctrine calls for the armor unit to be dropped with additional power cells and heavier extended-life power cells in their backpack units. Even so, they are designed for brief, intense firefights.

Users report that the A6 is inferior in comfort, operating range and power density to modern Manticoran or Solarian gear, but remains a powerful unit in combat, with near parity in armor protection and only somewhat inferior electronics.

ENLISTED UNIFORM AND BATTLE ARMOR

UNDRESS UNIFORM

BATTLE ARMOR

INSIGNIA

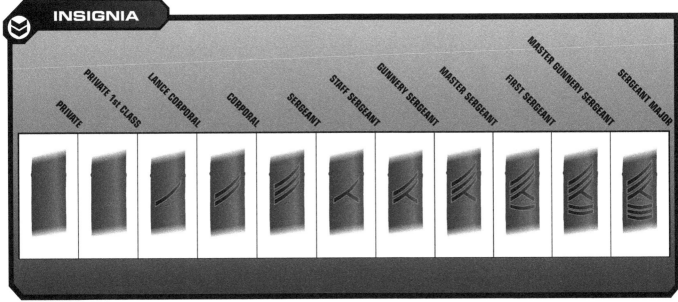

PRIVATE

PRIVATE 1st CLASS

LANCE CORPORAL

CORPORAL

SERGEANT

STAFF SERGEANT

GUNNERY SERGEANT

MASTER SERGEANT

FIRST SERGEANT

MASTER GUNNERY SERGEANT

SERGEANT MAJOR

L49 SERIES PULSE RIFLE

L49 Pulse Rifle

The L49 pulse rifle and its variants provide the standard shoulder arm for the People's Marine Corps, People's Army, Internal Security and local planetary police forces. It is a reliable weapon, designed for mass production with low overhead costs. By mating the standard receiver with a variety of parts, the rifle can perform in a number of different roles.

The L49 operates with a straight feed linear coil design providing reliable operation in a variety of conditions. Aside from the magazine and trigger assembly, the weapon contains no moving parts.

A standard magazine holds 98 darts in 4.7x53 mm caliber. Located behind the magazine is a standard issue C2500 power cell, which provides power for up to 300 rounds. Cyclic rate varies from 600 to 1200 RPM with a muzzle velocity of 1800 meters per second. A thumb selector can be used to switch between safe, semi automatic, burst and full automatic fire.

An electronic sight is attached to the mounting rail on the top of the weapon. The sight integrates with the weapon's data bus and can be operated in a variety of modes. A multipurpose dial is used to access various functions.

A common complaint with the initial L49 design was that the power cell could not be removed without first removing the magazine, a failing that has been remedied with the latest revision. The modified magazine well can accept both the older straight magazines as well as the newer reverse slanted magazines.

L49LG Support Rifle

The L49LG is a standard modification to the base pulse rifle, replacing the forward handgrip with 20mm grenade launcher. The launcher feeds from a 6-round box magazine and is capable of quick cycling semiautomatic fire. The launcher assembly is not field removable, but can be replaced with the proper tools in short order.

Standard issue grenade types are limited to high explosive (fuzed for impact, delay or airburst mode), incendiary and smoke. A number of nonlethal options are available to Internal Security units as the situation warrants.

Grenade fuzing is controlled by the toggle dial on the sight, which also displays windage, trajectory and estimated kill zones for the loaded round.

L49AB Battle Rifle

The L49AB is a variant of the standard L49 for use with battle armored troopers. The entire weapon is encased in an armored shell to protect it from the environment in which battle armor operates as well as the strength of the armor itself. The receiver is unmodified aside from the feed system, which has been adapted to fit a larger drum magazine.

The back side of the sight is covered by the same armored shell as the weapon, while data feeds are connected to the suit's heads up display through the handgrip. Similarly, the power system has been rearranged to allow the weapon to draw off the suit's internal power through the handgrip.

L49C Carbine

The L49C is designed for shipboard and other close quarters use. A short barrel is attached to the standard receiver, with the sight replaced by a simple reflex sight. To reduce weight, a D1200 power cell replaces the C-cell in the stock.

L49MS

The L49MS is rarely seen in naval or marine service, reserved for groundside use by InSec and police units. A short barrel contains a forward mounted connection for a D or Q cell while the standard stock is replaced by a lightweight telescoping variant. Like the L49C the full featured sight is eliminated in favor of a simple reflex sight.

L49 INTERNAL ARRANGEMENT

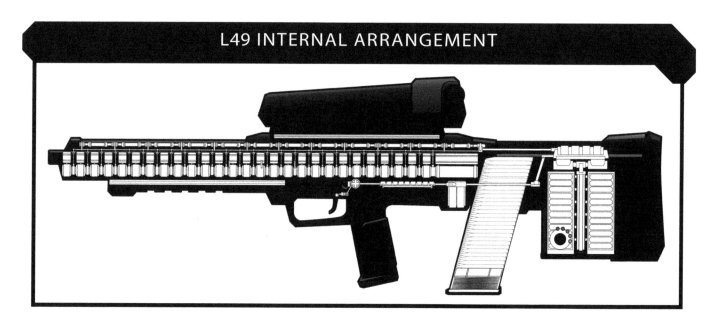

L49 SERIES - COMMON VARIANTS

Power Cells

L49 Pulse Rifle

Grenade Launcher

L49LG Support Rifle

L49AB Battle Rifle

L49MS SMG

L49C Carbine

1 ☐ = 25 Millimeters

D.450 *OURAGAN*-CLASS PINNACE

Specification

Mass: 283 tons
Length: 31 m
Wingspan (full extension): 24.3 m
Wingspan (folded): 20 m
Crew: 4
Capacity: 130 (22 passengers, 108 marines)
Power:
  RF/1 Phenix 2 Microfusion Reactor
Propulsion
  Small Craft Impeller Drive
  ER-7 Reaction Thruster System
  2 Dauphiné VT-13 Turbofans
Electronics
  AG-94 Gravitic Detection Array
  AR-95(b) Phased Radar Array
  BB-16 ECM Jammer
Armament:
  1 L/3 Light Antiship Laser
  2 TL27 25mm Pulse Cannon
  1 LM9(a) Missile Rack

Design and Construction

The Dauphiné D.450 *Ouragan*-class pinnace is the most common pinnace class in service with the People's Navy. The first units entered service in 1887 PD to replace the D.316 *Foudre*-class as the Navy's standard multirole transport.

The D.450 is capable of sustained atmospheric flight and maneuvers at speeds in excess of Mach four in standard 1 Bar atmospheres. The VT-13 turbofans can operate in pure air-breathing mode in atmosphere and provide the primary thrust for the reaction control system when sealed for exo-atmospheric operations. The impeller ring is covered by a series of baffles for atmospheric use. These baffles fold out of the way when the pinnace configures for impeller drive. The variable sweep wings can extend to a maximum wingspan of 24.3 meters for low speed flight and fold forward to a maximum oversweep of 20 meters for parking or docking in a standard boat bay cradle.

Like all small craft of the People's Navy, the D.450 is designed for longitudinal loading in the boat bay. This arrangement allows for efficient cargo transfer through the double-wide after hatch. Two side hatches in the forward quarter provide access to the cockpit and passenger bay. The impeller ring is mounted just forward of midships to allow free access to the cargo bay. The ring is oversized to allow for the passageway through the center, connecting the passenger deck to the cargo bay. The reactor, internal missile rack and other avionics equipment occupy this bay between the forward and rear habitable areas.

The D.450 has a crew of four; Pilot, Co-Pilot/Gunner and Communications Tech in the cockpit and a Flight Engineer's cubicle in the avionics bay. Just aft of the cockpit is the entry area, with a starboard side hatch and port side airlock, as is standard on Navy craft. A step up leads to the passenger bay, with seating for 22 and storage for a small amount of personal gear. Headroom in the forward section is limited due to the space taken by the dorsal gravitic bay. Another step up leads to the service passage through

the impeller ring and avionics bay to the cargo bay. A dog-leg accessway leads around the reactor and engineer's cubicle and a step down leads to the cargo bay.

Cargo capacity of the D.450 is six standard 290x220 cm pallets. The pallet system allows for a variety of modular cargo loads as well as various troop configurations as the mission requirements dictate. Maximum drop capacity in the bay is 108 marines with personal weaponry and gear, or 36 suits of A6 battle armor with support equipment and weaponry. The double-wide loading hatch allows for even multi-pallet loads to be moved onboard, though few warships have the boat bay space for such an operation. More commonly the purview of assault or cargo shuttles, pinnaces used by the People's Marine Corps and People's Army do occasionally get used to transport loads ranging from prefabricated buildings to skimmers or even light grav tanks.

The D.450 is armed with a pair of 25mm pulse cannon under the forward canards and a 3cm antiship laser centerline mounted under the nose. All three mounts are covered by armored panels during atmospheric reentry. Unlike its predecessor, the D.450 also mounts an internal missile rack on the starboard side of the midships bay. The rack can hold 4 Flèche tactical missiles with a variety of warheads and avionics packages. In addition to the internal armament, the *Ouragan* has on-wing hardpoints for an additional 17 tons of external ordnance.

IMPELLER CONFIG

D.450 TECHNICAL SPECIFICATION

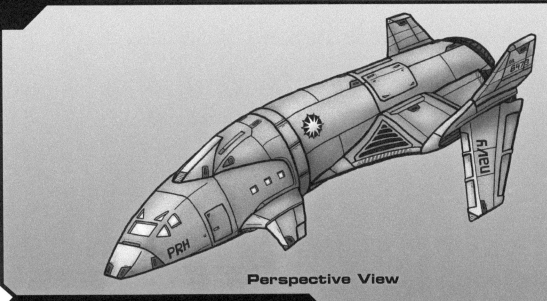

Perspective View

WING CONFIGURATIONS

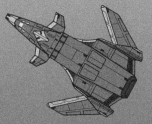

Atmospheric Flight

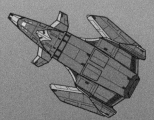

Boat Bay Docking

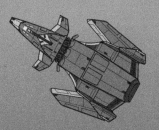

Impeller Configuration

HULL PROJECTION

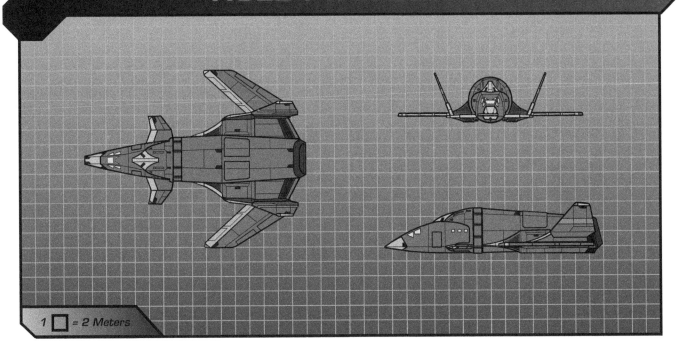

1 ☐ = 2 Meters

DR.41 *RAZZIA*-CLASS ASSAULT SHUTTLE

Specifications

Mass: 462 tons
Length: 63.1 m
Wingspan (full extension): 43 m
Wingspan (folded): 19.3 m
Crew: 6-8
Capacity: 250
Power:
  RF/1 Phenix 2 Microfusion Reactor
Propulsion
  Small Craft Impeller Drive
  ER-9 Reaction Thruster System
  2 Dauphiné VT-13 Turbofans
Electronics
  AG-93(a) Gravitic Detection Array
  AR-94 Phased Radar Array
  BB-15 ECM Jammer
Armament:
  2 TL27 25mm Pulse Cannon
  6 TL19 10mm Tribarrel Pulsers (2 each in 3 turrets)
Standard Equipment:
  F109 Camouflage Netting
  GP8 Heavy Grav Lifers
  64 sets AP7 Unpowered Body Armor
  80 cases Nou12 Survival Rations
Small Arms Racks (typical):
  30 M5 Pistols
  90 L49 Pulse Rifles
  80 L49LG Support Rifles
  20 L49C Pulse Carbines
  30 T17 Light Tribarrels
  5 T19 Medium Trbarrels
  10 P21 Plasma Rifles

Sufficient ammunition and power cells and spare parts are stored in the *Razzia's* storage bins to provide each weapon with 125% of a standard infantry load.

Design History

The Dauphiné-Roch DR.41 *Razzia* series Assault Shuttle has been in the service of the Republic of Haven with incremental upgrades for nearly 200 years. Designed with wings that fold back in to 19 meters to fit within a standard Havenite boat bay, the Razzia's full wing span is in excess of 40 meters when deployed.

Because Havenite boat bays are loaded from the ends, there is a design pressure on making the small craft that go into them long and narrow. The *Razzia* is roughly twice the length of the standard People's Navy pinnace and can fit into two adjacent standard boat bay berths if necessary. As this design constraint also works in favor of atmospheric speed without impellers, it's considered a win-win arrangement.

In configuration, the *Razzia* has a forward ramp, and two aft hatches with ramps for loading personnel and gear; for egress on a planetary surface, there are two side hatches to allow the troops to disembark rapidly. Because of the long, narrow cargo compartment, the *Razzia's* complement has to load their weapons into ready racks, rather than wear all their gear for the drop - this increases crew comfort for the trip into and through orbit and in the atmosphere, but does make assault drops a bit trickier. The full complement of a *Razzia* is 250 in drop configuration and *Razzias* operate in triplets, able to put a full battalion on the ground in one evolution.

The *Razzia's* armament includes twin 25mm pulse cannon in the forward mount, in addition to a turret meant for fire support and strafing ground targets. Over the two exit hatches are tribarrels mounted in dorsal turrets, to create a beaten zone. While not optimized for engaging in bombing missions, the vehicle mounts three hardpoints under each wing (for six total) to carry external ordnance pods. The craft is capable of high Mach values in most standard atmosphere regimes without gravitic assist, though this burns fuel prodigiously. For interplanetary drive capabilities, the *Razzia* mounts a solidly dependable impeller ring.

DR.41 WING CONFIGURATION

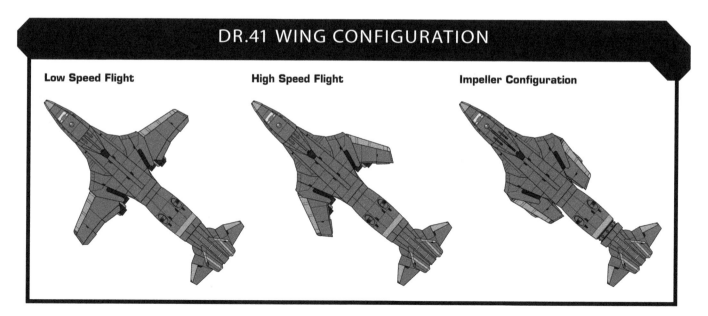

Low Speed Flight

High Speed Flight

Impeller Configuration

DR.41 TECHNICAL SPECIFICATION

Perspective View

HULL PROJECTION

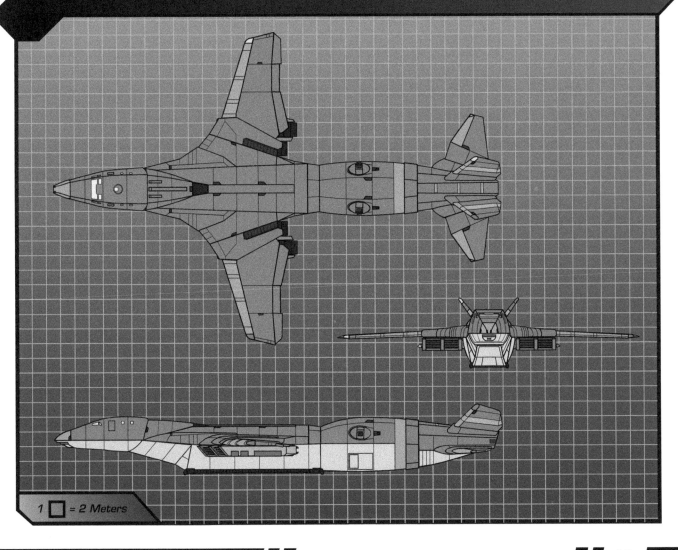

1 ▢ = 2 Meters

SAGANAMI ISLAND TACTICAL SIMULATOR

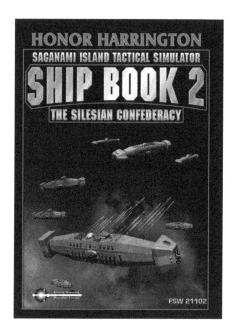

FSW21000   **Saganami Island Tactical Simulator**   **$74.95**
Space Combat in the Universe of Honor Harrington! Saganami Island Tactical Simulator (SITS) uses the critically acclaimed Attack Vector: Tactical game engine to put you in command of the ships of the Honorverse.

FSW21102   **SITS Ship Book 2: The Silesian Confederacy**   **$24.95**

FSW21103   **SITS Ship Book 3: The Short Victorious War**
$27.95

FSW21951   **Jayne's 1: The Royal Manticoran Navy**   **$29.95**

FSW21952   **Jayne's 2: The People's Republic Navy**   **$29.95**

www.finalswordproductions.com

MORE HONORVERSE PRODUCTS

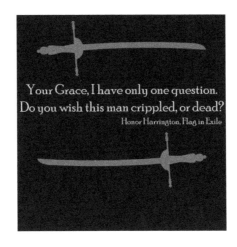

"Your Grace" T-shirt	**$20.00**
Royal Manticoran Navy T-shirt	**$20.00**
People's Navy T-shirt	**$20.00**
Royal Manticoran Marine Corps Window Cling	**$6.00**
Royal Manticoran Navy Window Cling	**$6.00**
Royal Manticoran Navy Embroidered Patch	**$10.00**
Royal Manticoran Marine Corps Patch	**$10.00**

www.finalswordproductions.com

CPSIA information can be obtained
at www.ICGtesting.com
Printed in the USA
BVHW021202250521
608002BV00011BA/2005